"After _____ own
at the homeless shelter,

there's no way I'm going to lose sleep over the damage at our fancy sorority house. We got a big fat insurance settlement. Every contractor came begging for the job. We'll have our fancy curtains and soft carpets back soon enough. The Tri Betas don't know how lucky they are, and I'm making it my job to show them."

KC impulsively grabbed Courtney's arm. "I just hope we don't lose you in the process."

"What difference would it make?" Courtney snapped. "I've made commitments to things that matter. Working at the homeless shelter, the soup kitchen, the tutoring program, has opened my eyes. There's more to life than credit cards and clothes and fancy furniture."

"But your own girls are homeless right now!" KC countered. "Doesn't charity begin at home?"

Don't miss these books
in the exciting FRESHMAN DORM series

FRESHMAN TABOO

LINDA A. COONEY

HarperPaperbacks
A Division of HarperCollins*Publishers*

Thanks to Dana Howard Botka

This is a work of fiction. The characters, incidents, and dialogues are products of the author's imagination and are not to be construed as real. Any resemblance to actual events or persons, living or dead, is entirely coincidental.

HarperPaperbacks *A Division of* HarperCollins*Publishers*
10 East 53rd Street, New York, N.Y. 10022

Copyright © 1993 by Linda Alper and Kevin Cooney
Cover art copyright © 1993 Daniel Weiss Associates, Inc.

Produced by Daniel Weiss Associates, Inc.,
33 West 17th Street, New York, New York 10011.

Cover illustration by Tony Greco

First printing: April, 1993

Printed in the United States of America

HarperPaperbacks and colophon are trademarks of HarperCollins*Publishers*

10 9 8 7 6 5 4 3 2 1

One

KC Angeletti's hands were shaking.

All she could do was grip the handle of her leather briefcase tightly and hurry down the charred hallway of her beloved Tri Beta sorority house.

Just keep moving ahead, she told herself, trying to block out images of the raging fire that had nearly trapped her.

But the nightmare wouldn't go away.

A few days before, someone had mysteriously thrown a firebomb into the Tri Beta sorority's living room during a jam-packed multicultural poetry reading. No one was seriously hurt, but parts of the elegant house had been destroyed. Worse, even the rooms that had escaped the flames were reeking of smoke, and all of the girls had had to move out.

KC was trying not to look at the blackened, gutted walls and shards of broken glass as she moved past the entrance to the grand living room. But there to the right was the gaping, splintered hole in the living room's picture window where the bomb had smashed through.

She paled, remembering the flash of light, the lacy curtains exploding into flame, the sting of smoke in her eyes, and the utter fear that she would never make it out in time.

"Makes you wonder, doesn't it?" KC heard a quiet voice behind her. It was pretty, soft-spoken Annie Neill, a Tri Beta sister headed to the same meeting on the sorority's back patio.

"Yeah." KC nodded, smoothing her long, dark hair and trying not to cry. "It—it scares me just to look at it."

"I know." Annie gazed absently at the gutted floor and collapsed near the grand piano. Her reddish hair floated casually about her shoulders, and her freckled, ski-jump nose made her look more like someone's kid sister than a talented art student already in her sophomore year. "Why would anyone want to do this? It doesn't make sense."

KC shook her head as she and Annie stared in disbelief at the depressing sight. Broken glass and overturned furniture were scattered throughout the living room. The once pale-blue curtains were now black, ragged, and still damp. The lovely oil painting over the mantel was lying facedown on the water-damaged, smoky carpet.

"I'm not sure," KC said nervously. All she knew was that the elegant, exclusive Tri Beta house didn't feel safe anymore.

"I have to get out of here," KC said suddenly, biting her lip and hurrying down the hall.

Annie followed. "Did you hear the sleeping porch was completely destroyed too?" she asked, her light step trying to keep up with KC's.

"Uh-huh," KC murmured, pressing her lips together tightly and pushing away thoughts of the fire as she turned into the dining room and rushed past a row of antique botanical prints. She couldn't think about it. She liked Annie and her friendly, freckled face, but she knew she couldn't think about the fire right now. If she did, she'd break down. And KC Angeletti—future businesswoman and the queen of control—never broke down in front of people.

The two girls made their way down the hall and out onto the back terrace. Outside, a group of Tri Betas, dressed in their usual elegant attire, was beginning to gather in the late Monday afternoon sun. It was the sorority's first full meeting since the disaster, and most of the girls looked as shocked and on edge as KC felt.

Murmuring a few hellos to their sisters, KC and Annie headed for a spot on the stone ledge overlooking the back garden's grassy slope. The tension in the air was so thick KC could almost hold it in her hands.

Tri Beta vice-president Diane Woo was staring forlornly at the blackened window frames. Freshman pledge Stephanie Bridgemont was weeping softly into a white handkerchief. Behind them, KC could see that half the lovely garden shrubs had been trampled in the fire-fighting effort. The lawn had been reduced to a grubby stretch of mud.

"How could this have happened?" KC whispered to herself. The Tri Beta house had been her fortress, her refuge, her strength. It had taken her through so much in the last few months: her father's death, her brief flirtation with drugs and alcohol, her money problems, her painful breakup with photographer Peter Dvorsky.

Its walls had always protected and comforted her. Now they were gutted and crumbling.

I've had enough destruction this year to last me for another ten, KC thought bitterly. *I just want everything back the way it was.*

KC settled in next to Annie, flicking a speck of lint off her well-worn black blazer and instinctively straightening her back. At least she had a happy, stable relationship. Campus-radio DJ Cody Wainwright had come into her life a couple of months before. And at least there was hope for her future business career. She was caught up on her college coursework, and her grades were rising. Even her friendships were thriving.

After checking her watch and offering a few anxious smiles to her gloomy sisters on the patio, KC looked up just as the French doors leading from the dining room burst open.

A slender girl with shiny blond hair and beautiful cola-brown eyes hurried out. It was Courtney Conner, the Tri Beta president—and one of KC's closest friends on campus.

"Hello, everyone!" Courtney said, cheerfully waving a handful of checks in the air. "The house renovation fund is getting larger by the minute. Look at these donations."

KC stirred uncomfortably. The Tri Betas were visibly upset, but Courtney was practically glowing with satisfaction. In fact, she looked happier and more filled with purpose than she had in a long time.

Diane gave Courtney a hard stare. "How can you be so chipper, Courtney?" she asked. "We've all lost precious belongings and our house is uninhabitable. Sure, we're lucky to have a wealthy alum like Mrs. Gomez lend us her house—but we can't camp there in our sleeping bags for much longer."

Courtney swiftly grabbed a patio chair and sat down in front of the assembled Tri Betas. She gave Diane a determined look. "No one was hurt in the fire, Diane. That's the important thing."

"But still—" freshman pledge Marcia Tabbert began.

"Look," Courtney interrupted, crossing her legs impatiently. KC stared at the unfamiliar pair of worn jeans Courtney was wearing, along with a neat but somewhat boring beige sweater. She'd never seen

Courtney wear anything but impeccably tailored clothes. "As far as I'm concerned, we're all lucky to be alive. We have our health and the money to rebuild. We have each other. What more could we ask for?"

KC winced. She knew what Courtney was saying. But how could her friend be so insensitive? Most of the Tri Beta girls were from wealthy, protective families. They'd never been through anything more traumatic than an unraveled hem or a bad blind date. *This* was major trauma time, and Courtney couldn't see it.

"Okay," Courtney began crisply, rolling a ballpoint pen between her thumb and forefinger with purpose. "Let's get to work."

A few of the girls glared at her.

KC felt her hand spring up into the air, almost before she knew what she wanted to say. "Courtney?" she blurted more sharply than she'd intended.

Courtney looked up, surprised. "Oh. Yes, KC?"

"Courtney," KC began carefully, trying to steady her voice. Suddenly her mouth was dry and her pulse was beating hard in her throat. "Um—it's just that I don't see anything wrong with acknowledging that we've all had a terrible scare. And—and that our lives are pretty much upside down right now."

"Good point, KC," Courtney said, unable to hide the edginess in her voice. "You're right, of course. I've been so wrapped up in our arrangements—I suppose I haven't—stopped to reflect." She pursed her lips and cleared her throat for attention. "The good news is that our insurance company has figured out the damages and will be delivering a check this week so our contractor can begin rebuilding the severely damaged sections of the house."

KC's eyes darted anxiously around the group. She noticed that a few of the girls were looking back at her, nodding in approval. In a way, KC didn't blame them for being irritated. Courtney was treating the fire like just another one of her worthy causes: protesting sexual harassment on campus, the Springfield soup kitchen, the Red Cross blood drive. Somehow, she'd managed to rope everyone else into her charitable infatuations.

It's been one thing after another, KC thought angrily. *She has great intentions, but the Tri Beta house is a social organization. Charities and causes should be left to personal choice.*

"Unless there are any objections, I will head the rebuilding committee," Courtney droned on like an efficient machine. "The insurance will cover construction and repairs, but unfortunately, it does not cover much of the cleanup work. I'll need volunteers right away."

KC watched as Courtney cheerfully whipped out two sign-up sheets fastened to clipboards.

"Why doesn't she just come out and say it?" Marcia whispered, ducking her head around the side of her lounge chair so that only those in back could hear. "She couldn't care less. Rebuilding the Tri Beta house is just another do-gooder project for her."

Diane, who was sitting next to KC, quietly nodded. Her black hair glinted in the late-afternoon sun. "She hasn't been the same since she dated that grubby news reporter who loves to tear apart the sorority-fraternity traditions in the campus newspaper."

A sophomore KC didn't know well leaned over. "Right. Dash Ramirez. Everyone knows he's the one who set the fire. Thank goodness he's in jail!"

KC shuddered inwardly. She knew Dash. He'd been the wrong guy for Courtney, but no one knew for sure that he threw the firebomb. It was one thing after another. Everything was out of control, and she hated it.

"At least this time the sign-up sheets are for our own house," Diane whispered, gazing irritably at her nails. "The poor and downtrodden will have to fend for themselves this week."

KC was wiggling her pencil nervously between two fingers. "Come on, Diane," she said in a hushed voice, "Courtney's always believed in community service. We've got to stand for something more than tea parties and frat dances, don't we?"

"Everyone, please," Courtney called out briskly. "I know many of you want to get your living situations squared away."

The Tri Betas turned forward with a hush.

"As all of you know, none of our rooms is livable right now. And they won't be for several weeks, during the cleanup," Courtney said, sliding her cool eyes about the group. "Mrs. Gomez can keep only a few of us on, because she's putting up a large group of exchange students from Brazil this week. The rest of you will need to make other arrangements."

There was an audible groan from the group.

"I've contacted the university housing office," Courtney continued. "It's going to allow those of you in the dorms to double up with one of your homeless sisters."

KC shifted, then gave Annie a shy smile. Annie's room had been smoked out.

"Those of you in the dorms," Courtney said matter-of-factly, "we need your help. Please try to pair up." Finally Courtney stood up to end the meeting. Her long neck rose proudly and her shoulders were squared, as if she were ready to fight. Her eyes traveled around the group, then stopped at KC.

"One final word, everyone," Courtney went on. "Everything's going to be all right. If we just approach this situation with courage and energy . . . well—I'm even sure something positive is going to come out of it."

KC closed her eyes in irritation, then turned to Annie just so she wouldn't have to look at Courtney. Still sitting wistfully on the stone ledge, Annie was gathering up her large square art portfolio, slipping a lock of curling hair over one ear. KC had always admired Annie's pretty features and the soft, arty style of her clothes. In a way, KC guessed, Annie was a little like herself. Different enough to stay on the outer fringe of Tri Beta life, but longing for friendship and stability.

"Well?" KC smiled at her shyly. "I've got a tiny place, but you're welcome to stay with me until you have your room back."

Annie's lively green eyes crinkled. There was a small space between her two very white front teeth—a tiny imperfection that made her seem all the more approachable. "Thanks, KC. I was hoping you'd say that."

KC smiled back, relieved. "Really?"

Annie touched KC's shoulder lightly with her slender hand, where a delicate silver bracelet dangled. Her gauzy, floral-design dress fluttered under a nubby jacket. "For a moment there, I thought Diane and Marcia were going to make me stay at Mrs. Gomez's. And I don't want to hear another word of complaint about how Courtney's turned into a do-gooder. I think Courtney's great."

KC stood up stiffly as the rest of the girls wandered into the house or down into the torn-up garden. "She is," KC said quickly. "Look, if you don't have a class, maybe we can walk over and see my room."

Annie laughed. "You mean it's ready for visitors on no notice? You must be terribly neat and tidy."

Linking her arm with Annie's, KC walked briskly into the house before Courtney had a chance to say anything to her. KC didn't know exactly why, but she didn't want to talk to Courtney now. She didn't want a pep talk. She didn't want to know how lucky she was. She just wanted to get out.

"Nope, I'm not especially tidy," KC explained,

stepping back out onto Greek Row, a wide, shady street lined with the largest sorority and fraternity houses. A few sleek cars roared by, and a group of women in bicycle-racing gear passed swiftly. "I'm just sort of strapped for money. I don't have enough possessions to clutter my room, no matter how hard I try."

"Well," Annie said, her light steps following KC down the street. "I'm a collector of junk—though a lot of it was damaged by the smoke."

"That's terrible."

Annie shrugged her slim shoulders. Then she pulled off her jacket and tied the arms casually around her waist as they crossed onto the campus and walked quickly past the boaters and sunbathers at Mill Pond. "It's okay. They're just things. Collecting experiences is more up my alley."

"That's something they don't teach us in Intro to Business," KC said bluntly. Then she flashed Annie a teasing smile. "Actually, I'm your typical business major. I lust after *things*. I long for stuff."

Annie giggled as they walked beneath a grove of spreading maple trees. With her jacket off, KC could see that Annie was very light and slender and covered all over with sprays of tiny brown freckles. With her swishing skirt, flickering earrings, and upturned nose, she almost looked as if she could float off on the next breeze.

"Well, I long for really *beautiful* things," Annie explained. "Special things. I'm an art-history major, you know. So I spend most of the day looking at wonderful paintings and sculpture—and trying to figure out what makes them so beautiful. My dream is to travel all through the world collecting art for a famous museum."

"I get it," KC said, stepping over a puddle. "And collecting a few adventures along the way."

"Exactly." Annie spread her slender arms wide and looked up at the sky. "The perfect job."

"Here it is." KC nudged her, pointing to a group of charming older houses with wooden porches. Lace curtains hung in the windows, and the neatly landscaped yards were dotted with bike racks, benches, and students quietly studying in the spring sunshine. "Langston House."

"Looks homey," Annie said with approval as KC pushed open the front door. Inside, the bulletin boards were crammed with announcements and messages.

"The Tri Beta house is my home," KC said abruptly, setting her jaw. "Or at least it was. This is just a quiet place to sleep and study. It's all-female, with a twenty-four-hour-quiet rule. I have probably the smallest room at the U of S, but it's all mine."

After climbing a wide staircase, KC led Annie down a narrow, carpeted hall to her door and unlocked it.

"Well, all mine most of the time," KC said, stepping inside. There, sprawled on his back on KC's bed, his nose in a thick novel, was KC's boyfriend, Cody. Dressed in his usual blue jeans, white shirt, and fringed leather vest, Cody looked just the opposite of the preppie-looking business-major type KC imagined she'd connect with in college. His shiny dark-brown hair was pulled back into a ponytail, and as he lifted himself politely up on one elbow, his caramel eyes began to lock on hers, just the way they always did.

"What are you doing here?" KC asked, surprised.

"Why—I—I—I'm snooping through your desk," Cody said teasingly, swiftly reaching one of his long arms out behind him. He slid a desk drawer open, pulled out one of KC's notebooks, and propped it up in front of his nose as if he were reading it. "Mmmm."

KC rolled her eyes and laughed.

"Annie, this is Cody Wainwright, who I guess has a key to my room, although I don't remember giving him one."

Cody dug into his pocket and held it up. "You did. Last week. In the library, when you asked me if I'd fetch your economics textbook from your room. Want it back?"

KC was trying to squelch her smile. "Cody?" she proceeded. "This is Annie Neill. She's going to stay with me until her room is fixed at the Tri Beta house."

"Hi." Cody stood up and shook Annie's hand politely. "Welcome to KC's palatial digs."

"I see what you mean," Annie said, looking around good-naturedly. She lowered her portfolio onto the floor. "There's barely enough room for KC's bed and desk in here as it is."

"Annie's got a point, KC. But we could move your desk a little. And I've got a cot over at my place I can lend. Maybe we can squeeze Annie in."

"There's no maybe," KC said, coolly folding her arms, trying not to look at Cody, who was making her prickle all over, just as he always did. "Unfortunately, Annie doesn't have the luxury of picking and choosing. Her beautiful room is gone and she needs a place. We'll be fine."

Cody surveyed the desk. Then he planted his cowboy boots and lifted it easily with his muscular arms.

"Yeah, that's the ticket," KC drawled, pushing the bed over. "Let's get going. Anything to distract us from the latest Tri Beta gossip. The way Diane and Marcia talk, you'd think Dash had firebombed the house for some vague reason having to do with that brief fling he had with Courtney."

Cody shook his head slowly. "Poor fella. Acts like a tough guy, but he's not. And it's Lauren Turnbell-Smythe he's crazy about. Shame he has to sit in jail like that."

"Well." KC kissed Cody quickly on the cheek. "I'll take your word for it."

Cody hooked her waist with his arm just as she was about to step away. Then he kissed her back and held his lips on hers a little longer, as if it were a tease or a challenge. For a moment, KC forgot that Annie was there. "I'll be seeing you now," Cody finally whispered in his soft Tennessee accent, giving the side of her face a swift, sweet stroke with his hand before he turned and left.

"Okay," KC whispered, catching her breath, still taking in the feel of his fingers. She turned to Annie and gave her an embarrassed shrug. "That's just Cody, I guess."

Annie was leaning against KC's desk, her arms crossed, a knowing look on her freckled face. "Uh-huh. He's the sort of guy who makes you want to forget all about the civil war that's smoldering over at the Tri Beta house. And I'm all for that. I can't stand the bickering. Life's too short."

"I know what you mean," KC agreed, suddenly flopping down on the bed that was still warm from Cody's body.

Annie laughed. "Anyway, speaking of living your life—don't worry about me. I don't want to get in the way."

"Oh, no . . ." KC tried to protest.

"KC," Annie said, hiking herself up casually on KC's desk and wrapping her curly hair into a bun on top of her head. "You and Cody have what you call *major* intensity. I can practically see the electricity in the air."

KC closed her eyes. She knew things were getting serious. Too serious. She loved Cody, but being near him was almost like fooling around with dangerous explosives. She was afraid to even think about lighting a match. Yet whenever he touched her, her body felt as if it were on fire.

"You're right," KC admitted, nervously pushing

a cuticle with her thumbnail. "But Woman does not live on electricity alone. I need good friends too—to help keep things cooled down."

Annie was staring at her thoughtfully.

KC sat up and headed for her closet, where she began pushing aside her few items of clothing to make way for Annie's. What KC wanted now was for everything to stay in place. For now, this room would have to be her safety net. She turned and looked at Annie.

"I'm really glad you'll be here. Cody and I need a little something between us for a while. We need more time to think."

"In that case, what you need isn't me," Annie said. "You need an iceberg."

Two

The front door to the Springfield city jail banged shut. Lauren Turnbell-Smythe felt a chill settle dully into her bones. She stared at the depressing signs on the concrete walls of the sparse waiting room.

NO FOOD. NO FIREARMS. NO WEAPONS.

For a moment, Lauren just stood there, staring stone-faced at the jail's main desk where an officer sat sternly in front of a sign-in sheet. For the past several days, the police had been holding her ex-boyfriend and fellow *Journal* reporter, Dash Ramirez, in connection with the Tri Beta fire. An hour ago, he had phoned to say his father had posted his bail and that he needed a ride back to campus.

Lauren drew herself up and narrowed her eyes, taking a deep, angry breath.

"Welcome to the U.S.A.," she muttered to herself, heading past a metal ashtray overflowing with cigarette butts. "Welcome to a country where innocent people are locked up for days on end without a hearing. Without evidence. Without cause."

"ALL PERSONS WHO PASS BEYOND THIS POINT ARE SUBJECT TO SEARCH," a sign read.

"Excuse me," Lauren said loudly to the police officer reading the sports page at the front desk. She pushed her wire-rimmed glasses up on her nose and stared hard at him. Already, her insides were beginning to turn. The stale tobacco and disinfectant smells were sickening.

The officer looked up.

"I'm here for Dash Ramirez," Lauren snapped, staring coldly at his metal badge. Didn't they understand? Dash had not started the Tri Beta fire. A bunch of dangerous, neo-Nazi skinheads had when they found out the sorority was hosting a black poet. Dash had been following them for a story, but when he found out about their ugly plans, he rushed to the Tri Betas to warn the crowd.

Now, Lauren fumed inwardly. Dash was the prime suspect, all because a bunch of spoiled frat boys wanted to pin the blame on him.

And the dangerous skinheads were still out roaming the streets of Springfield.

"Hi," she heard a gruff voice behind her. "You're here."

Lauren stuffed her hands into the pockets of her black jeans and turned around. It was Dash.

Just looking at him made her want to deliver a self-defense groin-chop to the entire criminal justice system. She could almost feel the smoke hissing out of her ears.

"Dash . . ." she began. "Dash, this is ridiculous. They can't do this to you. It'll destroy your whole life—your career . . ."

"Shhhh," Dash said softly, putting a hand up to her cheek and letting his black eyes settle into hers. "Not here."

Lauren couldn't unglue her eyes from him. Everything was so unfair. Dash's tawny skin was now a pasty white. His black hair was scragglier than ever. And his usual two-day stubble had turned into a ragged beard. She'd never seen him like this. Not even during their worst deadline crisis at the U of S *Weekly Journal,* when they stayed up for two straight nights drinking black coffee and eating nothing but microwaved burritos.

"Okay," Lauren agreed, clenching her teeth. She couldn't bear to spend another second in this place.

"Thanks," Dash muttered, heading toward the exit. He jammed the flat of his hand against the front door, pushed it open, then held it there for Lauren to go through. A bolt of love and indignation shot through Lauren. Part of her longed to throw her arms around him and say that everything was going to be all right, and another part remembered Dash's chauvinistic side, which had contributed to their breakup.

Lauren walked through the held door anyway. "I'm glad you called. What happened to your dad?"

"My big-shot, bank-president father didn't exactly enjoy coming down here and posting bail for me," Dash answered. He slung his leather jacket over his shoulder and shielded his eyes from the bright sunshine. "We got into an argument, and he took off."

"But Dash, he *did* post the bail."

"Yeah. But apparently my dad's got the Bill of Rights all mixed up," Dash began to blaze as he headed toward a shady table on the grass outside the courthouse-jail complex. "He's got some crazy idea that you're guilty until proven innocent."

Lauren tried to catch up with him. "What is wrong with everyone?" she cried out. "I don't get it, Dash. Why is everyone condemning you?"

"Maybe they don't like my Latino good looks," Dash snapped, thumping down onto the picnic table's bench and clasping his hands in front of him.

"But the police?" Lauren fumed. "Aren't they investigating? Aren't they trying to track down Billy Jones and his gang of neo-Nazi freaks?"

Dash smirked. "Let's just say they're not exactly breaking into a sweat over it." He jerked up his hand reflexively to his front pocket, where he usually kept a pack of cigarettes. There wasn't one.

Lauren sat next to him and stared furiously into space. She clenched her fists on her knees. "This is ridiculous. You've given them Billy Jones's address. Descriptions of the gang members. Everything."

"Yeah." Dash stuffed a rolled-up wad of gum into his mouth. "The cops did a routine investigation. They didn't find anything. They don't want to. They just want to say they tried, so they can go home to their safe little suburban tract houses and have a nice hot casserole dinner with their stupid wives. . . ."

Lauren slipped her arm into Dash's as he abruptly stopped, choking on his words. "Dash. If there's anything I can do, just say the word. I'm going to get you out of this." Lauren slipped her fingers protectively over a ragged spot on his worn jeans. Her heart was beating hard and she could barely swallow.

Slowly, Dash turned his face to her. "Thanks, Lauren. Sometimes I think you're the only one who's really thinking about me."

"I can't think about anything else!" Lauren burst out, half regretting it. She didn't know how ready she was to get this close to him again. All she knew was that Dash didn't deserve jail.

"Can't the police see that these punks didn't want inner-city poetry readings going on in lily-white Springfield?" Dash said in disbelief. He buried his face in his hands. "All I was trying to do was warn you and everyone else. For a moment, I thought you were trapped in there."

"I know."

"The police say they're going to keep digging," Dash murmured. "But what if they don't find them?"

Lauren stared glumly out at the Springfield traffic. A few kids were lazily chasing a dog near their table, and a man mopped his brow as he walked along the hot sidewalk.

"They will," she whispered, touching his hand. "They will."

Dash looked at her with his familiar black eyes and smiled for the first time. Lauren grew hot. She and Dash may have broken up months before. But as she sat there staring at him, she finally understood how much she loved and missed him. It was because of Dash that she became a writer. Because of his unselfish tip, she had just landed an internship at a new women's magazine. She had everything now, while Dash looked like a bankrupt soul.

Lauren began to tremble, but she was too scared to let Dash know how she felt. "Tell me where you need to go," she said abruptly, hopping off the picnic table. "I've got an appointment in fifteen minutes."

"Just take me over to the student union. I need to check in at the *Journal,*" Dash answered as he followed Lauren to her Jeep. He got in the passenger seat. "Where are *you* headed?"

"Remember the magazine internship?" Lauren walked around the car and slipped in next to him. "Today's my first meeting with the editor at *West Coast Woman.* Her name is Jamie Wells."

"Ah-*ha.*" Dash managed a smile as Lauren

merged into the traffic. "I spend a few days in jail while your career skyrockets."

"It doesn't feel right now, Dash," Lauren said hotly. "Now that you're in so much trouble."

"Well, at least it's a women's magazine," Dash joked. "You won't have to deal with all the sexism and chauvinism that's been bugging you lately."

"Drop it," Lauren barked. "Or you'll make me angry."

"Not so fast. Maybe once you're used to collaborating on stories with other feminist women, you may never want to write with me again," Dash quipped. "Of course, you might not get the chance if they throw me in the state pen—"

"That's not going to happen, Dash," Lauren cried out, punching the steering wheel with the heel of her hand as she pulled up in front of the student union. "Don't even think it."

Dash's face drew near hers, and for a moment Lauren thought he was going to wrap his arms around her. But suddenly she drew back, too confused and upset to know what to do or say. Now was not the time to get close to Dash again. Restlessly, she shifted the Jeep into gear.

"Thanks," Dash mumbled, opening the car door and slipping out. "See you around."

Lauren stepped on the accelerator and swerved into the traffic, her mind crackling with anger and confusion. By the time she'd returned to downtown Springfield, she was having trouble finding a parking space. Her khaki blouse was sticking to her back and her hair was slowly frizzing up into a major buzzball.

"Dash Ramirez. Capable of throwing firebombs into a house full of people. Right," she whispered sarcastically. She slipped the Jeep into a spot, jumped out, and jammed some coins into a meter. "Just try to prove it to a jury."

Lauren hurried down the sidewalk until she reached the lovely stone entrance of an historic building that had been turned into street-level shops and upstairs offices. After climbing a flight of stairs, she stopped in front of a classy glass-and-oak door that read WEST COAST WOMAN in thin, black letters. Taking a huge breath, Lauren walked in.

The office was spare, yet chic. Sleek framed posters had been carefully hung on white walls, and the open-air editorial area was punctuated by elegant columns and lush indoor plants. Sunshine fell through the skylights onto the no-nonsense gray carpeting and white desks.

Lauren waited patiently in the reception area, watching the women staffers consulting over page layouts, talking on the telephone, and furiously typing on computers.

West Coast Woman wasn't any ordinary rag, Lauren reminded herself. It was a new, highly acclaimed regional magazine, known for its exposés on women's issues, profiles of successful women, business, and even fashion. For her internship, Lauren was going to research and write one major article.

Finally a woman with curly, shoulder-length hair and exotic-looking earrings hurried up to the desk, carrying a thick stack of manila folders and a cup of coffee. "Sorry," she muttered through a pencil that was lodged in her mouth. She set the load down and slipped the pencil behind her ear. "It's been a crazy day. One emergency after another."

Lauren gave her a stiff smile. "Oh. It's okay. I'm used to craziness." She extended her hand politely. "I'm Lauren Turnbell-Smythe from the U of S *Weekly Journal*."

"Oh, you're our new intern. Nice to meet you."

A few heads popped up and nodded with appreciation. Lauren warmed. She knew that Dash wanted this for her. He'd found out about the internship and had told her about it. It was his gift, and it was up to her to succeed.

Another woman approached Lauren from a light table in back. Her straight gray hair was cut in a fashionable bob, and her ethnic-print skirt swished as she walked. "Hello, Lauren," she said with an extended hand. "I'm Jamie's assistant editor, Toni Wallerstein. Welcome to our humble abode. Jamie is really looking forward to meeting you. We loved your tryout piece on self-defense training."

"Oh, thanks," Lauren replied in a daze. "But this place isn't exactly humble. You should see the cave we work in on campus."

Toni gave a hearty laugh and guided Lauren through the brightly lit maze of open work spaces.

She ducked her head into a large office in the corner, partitioned off from the main room but outfitted with large windows. "Jamie! Lauren's here," Toni called out casually, patting Lauren on the shoulder. "Go right in. It won't be a moment."

Lauren smiled and headed in the door. Immediately, her heart began to sink.

Her new boss wasn't *Ms.* Jamie Wells. It was *Mr.* Jamie Wells.

Lauren stared.

"Yeah, yeah," Jamie was agreeing over the phone, looking up at Lauren and motioning for her to sit down. Instead of the warm, sophisticated woman she'd expected, Jamie was a blond-haired guy in his late twenties with a stocky build and wire-rimmed glasses. The sleeves of his white business shirt were rolled up, and his arty-looking tie had been loosened. He looked more like a tough prosecutor than the editor of a women's magazine.

She sat down in the chair facing him and shifted uncomfortably.

"Let's wait on the lumberjack women story until Daria has her facts cleared up with the Forest Service—and with just about all her other sources, for that matter. Yeah."

It was infuriating, Lauren thought hotly. A women's magazine staffed entirely by women, but headed by a *man*? It was outrageous. She wanted to scream. She wanted to overturn one of his tasteful potted plants with one of her self-defense kicks. What was going on in the world? An innocent man can be jailed for days without a hearing? A women's magazine can be dictated to by a guy?

"Okay," he snapped into the telephone, his green eyes moving over to her every few seconds as if he wanted to talk to her instead of the person on the line.

Finally he slammed down the phone and stood up abruptly, extending his hand across his cluttered desk. "Hello, Lauren. Glad you're here."

"Um, yes," Lauren murmured, wincing. His handshake was so hard and enthusiastic, he was practically breaking her knuckles. She pulled away and sat back down.

Without warning, Jamie grabbed a sheet of paper off his desk and thrust it at her. "You've seen the description of the internship, so you know we'll need you to write one full-length article," he continued gruffly. "We've got a great staff and a good publication, so you should be happy. We liked your tryout piece, by the way."

"Great," Lauren snapped back, waiting for him to ask her to get coffee, or inquire about her typing speed.

"I've compiled a list of story ideas for you to look over," Jamie said, interrupting her thoughts.

Lauren glanced down at the sheet of paper, then clenched her jaw. He might as well have asked her to pour him some coffee. The story ideas were insulting.

"Mixing and matching linens," she murmured to

herself in disbelief. "Low-maintenance gardening. The well-organized desk. Snappy meals for under five dollars."

Lauren felt her skin crawling with disgust. Did these people actually think that she wanted the internship so she could write fluff pieces for bored people in dentists' offices? Is this the kind of story she'd been training for all year at the *Journal*?

"We'll get together again ASAP," Jamie barged ahead, "and decide on your topic."

"But . . ." Lauren started to protest.

Lauren watched as Jamie stood up behind his desk and rubbed his hands together. His eyes roved the piles of paper until he spotted what he was looking for and grabbed it. "I apologize for cutting this short, Lauren. But it's been one of those days," he grunted before hurrying out.

"You bet," Lauren whispered to herself, still sitting in the chair in shock.

After a moment, Lauren hiked her book bag up on her shoulder and ran her fingers irritably through her wispy blond hair. Now she understood why Jamie wanted an intern. He probably wanted to save the hard-hitting investigative articles for himself, so he needed someone to write the mindless homemaking and gardening topics he stupidly thought women bought the magazine for.

With the grunt work out of the way, Lauren fumed, Jamie would be able to focus on the good stuff and take all the glory for himself.

Lauren felt sick. In a way, she was just as much a prisoner as Dash had been in the city jail. A prisoner of her sex. A prisoner of the way the world looked at her—and every other woman on the planet.

Three

....

"**A**h, a beautiful day in the lovely mountain town of Springfield," Faith said as she and her best buddy in the theater department, Merideth Paxton, headed down the campus pathway toward the student union building. Both wanted a career in the theater—but not as actors. They both longed for the backstage life as directors, stage managers, designers, or producers. "It's good to be around friends again," Faith added.

Merideth nodded. "Haven't seen much of you lately. Someone said you had a heavy boyfriend."

Faith cringed.

"Oooh," Merideth teased as they strolled past a

large fountain. "Does boyfriend spell problem or blessing?"

"Maybe a little of both," Faith said. "Becker *was* pretty isolating. I guess philosophy majors are loners by nature. So things have cooled off—for good."

"Look on the bright side," Merideth pursued, bouncing a little on his sneakers. "You're free to be all high and mighty, now that you've been accepted into the Professional Theater Program."

Faith stopped in the middle of the path. "Get serious," she scolded. A few weeks before, Faith had applied to and been accepted by the U of S's prestigious program for theater students. Next fall, Faith would be one of the youngest in a select group of experienced upperclassmen and graduate students involved in small seminars led by top-notch professionals in the field.

Merideth grinned. "Aw, heck. I'm just jealous. I didn't even have the guts to apply."

"Forget it," Faith mumbled. "I was pretty self-absorbed there for a while."

"Like a sponge she was," Merideth mocked, dabbing the air. "Mopping up her own emotional juices . . ."

Faith playfully bumped into Merideth's side, reached up, and clamped her hand over his mouth. "What I'm trying to say . . . is that I miss everyone. I'm sick of thinking about myself and my all-important career. Becker didn't care about anyone but himself, and I got that way too for a while."

"So now?"

"Now . . ." Faith was feeling bouncy, free and loose. "Now I just want to get my old life back. My old friends. KC, Winnie, Lauren . . . you."

"Good," Merideth said. "And I've got just the thing for your aching heart. It starts in five minutes."

"What is it?" Faith demanded, pushing open the front door of the student union. Two guys were struggling to carry a kayak through the door, while students loaded down with heavy book bags swirled around them like stream water.

Merideth suddenly looked as if he'd lost himself in a far-off thought. "You'll see. Come on upstairs to the ballroom. There's a meeting."

When they reached the top of the stairs, Faith saw that the ballroom was packed with students. But as Merideth led her through the crowd, it wasn't clear what the meeting was about. All she could tell was that the mood was strangely quiet—almost solemn.

Faith took in the atmosphere. Just about every campus type was there. Backpackers. Clean-cut types from the science and math departments. Women in suits. Younger girls with dyed red hair and black leather jackets. A large group of her friends from the theater department were milling around the front podium.

"Hey," Merideth spoke up, yanking Faith ahead. "Robert."

Faith stepped forward to see a clean-cut-looking guy wearing a red flannel shirt and new-looking jeans. His blue eyes had a friendly twinkle under his dark eyebrows, and his brown hair was clipped short. Faith smiled. Although the guy had obviously wetted down the top of his head, his hair stood stubbornly on end. A neat-looking backpack hung from one of his broad shoulders.

"You're here," the guy said with relief, gripping Merideth's upper arm briefly. "Go get 'em."

"Okay," Merideth said distractedly. "Oh. Faith, this is Robert. Robert, Faith."

Faith smiled fleetingly at Robert's wholesome, L.L. Bean–catalog good looks. Then she watched with bewilderment as Merideth snaked through the crowd and finally took the microphone. She gave a little gasp.

Merideth was conducting the meeting.

"Hi, folks," Merideth said in a low voice. His face was suddenly pale, and the Adam's apple on his long neck was nervously bobbing up and down. "Thanks for coming. This is attention time for an extremely important and urgent topic."

Faith looked in wonder at Merideth. His expression had dropped now to deadly serious as he scanned the room.

"AIDS," Merideth said loudly and simply into the mike.

A wave of silence rippled through the jam-packed room.

"AIDS," he repeated softly.

For a few terribly long and painful seconds, the room was as quiet as a tomb. Faith looked up at

Merideth. He was standing perfectly still, his arms hanging at his sides, his eyes gazing fearlessly over the crowd. All around her, students were nodding their heads quietly, as if they were taking a moment to say a silent prayer.

"It's a powerful word—isn't it?" Merideth finally continued. Faith watched him, unable to breathe. In his eyes was a focus and a fire that was connecting with every last person in the room. She could almost feel the physical solidarity of the group. Arms were linked together. Hands were clasped. Looks were shared.

"Last winter, a friend of mine died from this cruel disease," Merideth continued. He leaned forward on the podium and looked sternly at the crowd. "His name was Colin. Colin was a good person. The kind of generous, caring person anyone would want to have for a friend. He was a premed student, I might add. Headed for great things."

Faith froze.

Colin.

She remembered now. Last winter, during *Macbeth* rehearsals, Merideth was stage manager. He'd been looking tired. She remembered how he'd show up with red eyes, and the odd way he'd seem to forget props, almost as if he were living in another world. Then there was that day. The day they were rehearsing Lady Macbeth's death scene: *Life's but a walking shadow, a poor player that struts and frets his hour upon the stage and then is heard no more . . .*

Faith drew her hands up to her mouth in horror, remembering the way Merideth had broken down in front of her as he sat on a stool backstage. She'd wanted to help. She'd wanted to ask him about it. But their temperamental director, Lawrence Briscoe, had come storming in, asking for quiet on the set, and Merideth had rushed out the backstage exit.

"Oh, my God. I'm so sorry, Merideth," she whispered to herself. "I didn't know. I was so busy with everything . . . and then I guess I just forgot."

"Colin is the reason I organized this meeting today," Merideth continued. The group was so silent and together that it was beginning make Faith's heart break. She took another tiny peek around. Two women in baggy pants stood together, sniffing. Others had bent their heads down. In the background, she could hear quiet coughs and murmurs. "It's time we did something together to help people like Colin who are suffering. His parents did. In fact, they organized Springfield's first AIDS hospice, and named it Colin's House."

Someone cleared her throat. In the back, a door banged.

"I'm proposing a fund-raiser to help support Colin's House," Merideth said urgently. "It's an epidemic, folks. Right now, at least one million people in the United States are believed to be infected with the HIV virus. Nearly a quarter of a million people have come down with AIDS—which, so far, is incurable."

Faith gulped.

Merideth straightened up. "More than five thousand fifteen- to twenty-four-year-olds have died of AIDS in this country. That's us, folks. And it's not just a gay disease. Look at the figures. Right now, twelve percent of the people in that age group who have AIDS are straight."

"We've got to educate people," a girl from the U of S track team murmured, shaking her head.

"Students here need to know how to avoid getting the disease," Teresa Gray, head of the off-campus Crisis Hotline, spoke up. She was perched on the edge of a dusty ballroom table, a pencil stuck into her frizzy bun. "And they need to be more aware about how they *can't* get it. I've got kids calling the hotline at all hours, scared to death that they've caught it from a handshake with a gay person. Or from a toilet seat. The fact is, you get the disease through unprotected sex, a transfer of blood—such as IV needle sharing, and from mother to fetus. The misconceptions are pretty horrible."

Merideth nodded, slipping the mike out of its stand and walking over to a nearby chair. He sat down and rested his gangly elbows on his knees. "We need to educate. I completely agree." His eyes scanned the audience again and rested briefly on Faith. "Everyone with me?"

A ripple of approval threaded its way through the crowd. Faith felt her heart climbing up inside her throat as she looked at Merideth. Before this moment, AIDS had been a distant, terrible disease she occasionally read about in the newspaper. Now it felt very near. Very real.

"Any fund-raiser ideas?" Merideth asked, his dark eyebrows rising hopefully.

"The gloom-and-doom approach doesn't work," called out one of the theater department's top actors. "People get turned off."

"How about an auction?" a girl piped up.

"A race of some kind?" a guy in a sweatshirt suggested. "Like a marathon or a bike race?"

Faith frowned. Standing on tiptoe, she looked around the room at the blank faces. People were standing around, or lounging on the stacked-up ballroom chairs, talking quietly to one another, looking confused. Then her eyes settled on a large, leotard-clad group from the dance department. Suddenly, it hit her.

"How about a danceathon?" Faith heard herself say.

A dozen people turned to look at her.

"Not bad." Merideth nodded. A slow, sad smile turned up a corner of his mouth. "I like it."

All eyes were on Faith now. "I organized a danceathon in high school," Faith went on, realizing that everyone was waiting for her to explain. "It was a huge shindig—but a pretty serious competition, too."

Faith watched as her dancer friends' eyes lit up. The sadness in the room began to fade a little. She stepped shyly onto a low stack of exercise pads on the side of the room, so that the group could hear her.

"People paid to get in," Faith spoke up, "but we also charged for participation in each individual dance contest." Faith put her hand to her forehead, trying to remember the dances. "Uh—we had jitterbug, swing, sixties rock, Charleston, waltz. It was—fun."

Faith breathed more easily, bolstered by the sea of nodding heads that hadn't taken their eyes off her. Whispers of approval floated up. Merideth was smiling and shaking his head, his hands on his hips. "Somehow, I just knew you'd come to the rescue, Faith."

"You'll need a lot of publicity, of course," Faith explained. "But I know my friend Melissa McDormand and her cartoonist friend, Danny Markam, would make posters. Winnie Gottlieb down at the hotline could do the promotion and education from that end. And my friends Kimberly Dayton and Liza Ruff, who have a great feel for good dancing and entertainment, could do some of the judging. . . ."

"Everyone in favor of the danceathon idea," Merideth called out, now standing on his chair, "say aye."

"AYE."

"Done," Merideth said with authority. "Sign-up sheets are in the back! Thank you, everyone, for coming. It's going to make a difference."

Faith's blood was churning in her veins. For a moment, she just stood on the exercise pads, breathing hard, wondering if she should burst into tears or laughter. There was a strange mixture of sadness and friendship in the room that she couldn't quite get a handle on. She hadn't been prepared for it.

Stepping down into the crowd, Faith began moving patiently toward Merideth. She wanted to talk more about the fund-raiser. The meeting had been moving and serious, and it had sparked something positive in her. She'd found something she'd been looking for, something to pour herself into. She gripped her book-bag strap tighter. If her disastrous relationship with Becker had taught her one thing, it was that she wasn't a loner. She was a giver.

"Hey," Merideth called out, breaking away from a group of friends. He hugged Faith tightly, then pushed her away a little, holding on to her shoulders. His face was flushed and his dark curls were glistening with sweat. "Thanks."

Faith slipped her hand wordlessly onto his shoulder. But his eyes suddenly disconnected and fell into the crowd behind them. She felt him pull away. His face looked urgent, then soft. He was reaching out to hug someone. Faith stepped away.

It was Robert.

For a moment, Faith just stood there, waiting for Robert's congratulatory hug to end, so she could drag Merideth out for a cup of coffee to discuss her idea.

But the hug lasted.

Taking a slight step back, Faith watched as Robert's strong hand remained on Merideth's shoulder. The muscles in his square jaw were clenched and his blue eyes seemed to be delivering some unspoken message. Then he leaned over and said something softly into his friend's ear, causing both of them to chuckle softly. Suddenly, Faith realized that the two were in their own world.

She blushed.

Merideth and Robert weren't casual friends. They were a couple.

"Um," Faith spoke up, looking self-consciously around the nearly empty room. A metal door gave a hollow bang in the distance. She began to back up. "Let me know when you want to meet on this, Merideth."

"Yeah, okay," Merideth called out as Faith began to hurry toward the door. "Hey, thanks again, Faith."

Faith let the door crash behind her and stepped quickly down the student-union stairway. She didn't know why she was feeling so embarrassed. After all, she knew Merideth was gay. They'd talked about it a lot.

It was just that she'd never actually seen him with another guy.

Faith pursed her lips, irritated with herself.

Sweet little Faith from small-town Jacksonville, Faith thought, bolting across the street and onto the campus pathway. *Good old Jacksonville, where homosexuality exists, but is never discussed openly. You're an adult now, Faith.*

"Grow up," she scolded herself.

Four

....

KC wedged her crowbar under the edge of the smoky carpeting in the Tri Beta's main hallway and began pulling the pad up from the row of sharp nails.

"Uuuuugggghhhh," she grunted, pushing a wisp of dark hair off her forehead. "Five more feet to go and we're done."

It was Tuesday midafternoon at the Tri Beta house. Courtney had arranged a picnic lunch in the still-uninhabitable house, followed by a mandatory afternoon work party. KC sat up on her knees and looked around with a glow of satisfaction. Courtney could have easily skipped making it required labor. Never before had KC seen her sorority sisters so together—so determined to bring back their home to its former glory.

All around her, the house buzzed with activity. Vacuums whirred. Nails pounded. Even the most refined girls had abandoned their velvet headbands and shirtwaists for jeans, and all were busily plunging scrub brushes into pails of harsh detergents.

It made KC feel proud to be a Tri Beta.

"Four, three, two, one," Courtney counted down as the carpet popped up. "Bingo!" she murmured, sitting back on her heels. Dressed in faded blue jeans, a denim shirt, and with a red bandanna around her head, KC decided Courtney looked more like a factory worker than a sorority president from one of the wealthiest families in Oregon.

KC smiled at her friend. If it hadn't been for Courtney, KC never would have made it into the sorority. Courtney had never cared that KC was an Angeletti and not an Argyle or an Anderson. Despite the objections of some of the snootier Tri Betas, Courtney hadn't cared that KC's family was barely scraping by as the owners of an organic restaurant.

Courtney was the one who'd opened doors for her.

"Okay," Courtney said abruptly, standing up and checking her watch. Then she raised her voice and squared her shoulders. "I'm going to be leaving now, everyone. I'm due for volunteer work at the Springfield community center."

Diane Woo's scrub brush stopped in midair. A look of disbelief swept across several tired faces in the hallway. "You can't leave," Diane said, stunned. "We've got days of work ahead of us. We need to get our house back in order, Courtney."

Courtney wiped her hands matter-of-factly on the front of her jeans. "Nevertheless, I have a commitment to tutor a group of disadvantaged kids twice a week, and I'm not going to let them down."

Marcia Tabbert glared. "I don't believe—"

"In fact," Courtney interrupted, her smooth skin and clear eyes shining with conviction, "the program needs more volunteers. Would a few of you be willing to join me?"

A hush settled over the room, and there were blank looks all around.

"Come on." Courtney smiled the same smile she used in formal reception lines and alumni teas, her delicate hands poised on her hips. "The kids are wonderful. And they need our help so badly. We'll get the house finished soon enough."

"Courtney," Diane complained, rolling up a grimy, sagging cuff on her work shirt. "We're exhausted. Half of us have pulled muscles and dropping grade-point averages thanks to the work we're putting in here. Now you want us to drop everything before we're done and run off to another project?"

KC looked around at her sisters' weary, ragged faces. Diane was right. Courtney was out of line. Everyone was burned out from all the wallpaper peeling, painting, and cleanup. Now she wanted to make them feel guilty about the misfortunes of others? It was unfair.

"I'll join you, Courtney," KC heard herself say, glancing coolly around the circle of confused Tri Betas. After the last meeting, she knew everyone assumed she and Courtney were feuding. But they weren't. And she didn't want anyone to think they were. Even if she did disagree with Courtney right now.

KC stood up and placed her crowbar on a nearby sawhorse.

"That's the spirit, KC. I'll check in with the rest of you later," Courtney said. She linked arms with KC and led her cheerfully down the hall toward the front door. KC cast a guilty look over her shoulder. A few of the girls were shaking their heads in disgust. Others were ignoring them completely.

It wasn't until KC stepped out into the broad sunshine that she realized how weary and irritable she'd become from hours of renovation work. Her neck was stiff, her arms ached, and her skin felt itchy from plaster dust. But she knew she had to talk to Courtney.

"I think we made a lot of progress today," Courtney chirped, beaming at the thick archway of leaves floating above them as they hurried down Greek Row. "But I just can't wait to see my kids. Some of them have it so bad at home . . . I can scarcely believe they have the energy to make it down to the program after school."

KC stared. Courtney was in deep space and someone had to bring her down to earth before she zoomed out of orbit. The only problem was, would Courtney end up seeing KC's criticism as a threat—or an act of loyalty?

"Duck over to the post office with me, KC," Courtney ordered, rubbing her neck. "We're getting our mail delivered there for now." She looked at KC conspiratorially as they walked down the main boulevard toward downtown Springfield. "You're awfully quiet. Carpet-ripping got you down?"

KC shrugged, panting to keep up with Courtney's brisk pace. Courtney seemed more excited about a group of strange kids than she was about solving the Tri Beta's currently desperate housing situation. Plus, she appeared to be blissfully unaware that she still had dirt all over her face and that her golden hair was completely hidden under a red banana.

"I'm worried, Courtney," KC ventured, twisting an end of her long hair. She wanted to be careful.

Courtney's beautiful, smudged face looked wistful. She slipped her hands into the pockets of her jeans and stepped into the crosswalk, heading off-campus. "What about, KC? Boyfriend? Home?"

"I'm worried about you," KC said bluntly.

Courtney's laughter rose above the sounds of rushing traffic. "Really."

KC set her jaw. Someone had to tell her. "I don't think you understand. A lot of the girls are very upset about all of your outside activities."

"I realize that."

KC hurried to keep up as they passed the gracious

Peabody Mansion, with its lovely lawns and rose hedges. "It's the fire, Courtney. Everyone's lives are upside down. We need you. We need to put the house back in order. You shouldn't have left the work session the way you did."

"I had a commitment," Courtney said sternly. "Tutoring disadvantaged kids is important. They're counting on me, and I'm not going to let them down."

"I admire what you're doing. And the older girls would never criticize you," KC said. "But the younger ones don't understand. And they're talking. They don't trust you to do what's best for the sorority anymore."

"Look," Courtney barked, stopping in front of a busy gas station. A car bumped noisily past them as it pulled in, but Courtney seemed unaware. Her untucked denim shirt flapped messily in the breeze, and her brown eyes looked unfamiliar and sharp. "I know that many of the girls blame the fire on me. They've got some crazy idea that because I dated Dash—and because Dash was unjustly arrested for trying to help us—that it's somehow my fault. But I'm not going to honor that idea with a reaction. It's ridiculous!"

"That's just it. You have to show them that the rumors are false. You have to be a strong leader, now more than ever."

Courtney shook her head, storming ahead. "After what I've seen down at the homeless shelter, there's no way I'm going to lose sleep over the damage at our fancy sorority house. We got a big fat insurance settlement. Every contractor came begging to do the job. We'll have our fancy curtains and soft carpets back soon enough. The Tri Betas don't know how lucky they are, and I'm making it my job to show them."

KC impulsively grabbed Courtney's arm. "I just hope we don't lose you in the process."

"What difference would it make?" Courtney snapped, narrowing her eyes and staring straight into KC's. "I've made commitments to things that matter. Working at the homeless shelter, the soup kitchen, the tutoring program, has opened my eyes. There's more to life than credit cards and clothes and fancy furniture . . ."

"But your own girls are homeless right now!" KC countered, following Courtney across the street to the steps of the historic post-office building. "Doesn't charity begin at home?"

Courtney shook her head in exasperation, running up the stairs. KC caught the back swing of the heavy metal-and-glass door and followed her inside. Then she breathed. The air was blissfully cool, and the old-fashioned high ceilings and quaint directional signs were calming. She watched impatiently as Courtney opened the Tri Betas' post-office box and pulled out a large stack of mail, then sat down on a shiny wooden bench to sift through the envelopes.

"Oh, look," Courtney murmured, ripping open a small pink envelope with a subtle raised monogram. "It's good old Mrs. Wiley. What a sport." Courtney read her letter eagerly as a check dangled casually from her fingers. "She's sending us three thousand dollars to help fix up the Tri Beta house. We can use it any way we want, but—get this, she's so wonderfully eccentric, she suggests we use it to build a *gazebo* in the backyard. Can you imagine being so frivolous when so many children go hungry?"

KC was speechless for a moment. She followed Courtney out the double doors into the sunshine, all the while thinking about her Tri Beta sisters and the devastated sorority house. "I don't know," she pointed out. "It would sure do a lot to lift everyone's spirits."

Courtney sighed. "Maybe I am being too hard. Maybe we should pamper our—"

"KC!" came an ear-splitting scream at the end of the sidewalk.

KC turned around and paled. Racing toward them in her orange running tights, purple halter top, and hot-yellow Walkman headset was Winnie Gottlieb, one of KC's best friends from high school. KC's heart sank. Winnie worked at the off-campus Crisis Hotline and had a knack for sniffing out volunteer types.

"Hi!" Winnie yelled, gaily waving a red and blue flyer. Her backpack appeared to be loaded down with many more. "Hot off the presses. AIDS-prevention tips," she bubbled. "We're setting up an AIDS-prevention program at the hotline in connection with the big fund-raiser we're doing for Colin's House, the AIDS hospice. Have you heard about it?"

"An AIDS fund-raiser?" Courtney asked eagerly,

her cheeks flushing. KC looked suspiciously between Winnie and Courtney, tapping the tip of one patent-leather flat on the warm sidewalk.

Winnie nodded and readjusted the pack on her back. Her dark hair stuck out all around her head in little spikes, and she was chewing a wad of purple bubble gum. "Yeah. Isn't it great? Faith thought of the idea of a danceathon, with proceeds going to Colin's House," Winnie rattled on. "Anyway, my job is to educate, educate, educate. It's incredible how many people are getting sick just because they don't know much about it. A lot of kids think you can get AIDS only if you're gay. But did you know that in the last three years, the total number of thirteen- to twenty-four-year-old heterosexuals diagnosed with AIDS increased by seventy-seven percent?"

"That's terrible," Courtney gasped. "I had no idea it was that bad."

"Oh, it's a terrible problem," Winnie went on, "because so many teenagers don't even want to think about safe sex. They just seem to think they're *immortal* or something. It's time they woke up and realized that AIDS is a real killer and—"

"Um, well, good luck with the fund-raiser," KC broke in. "Cody and I are going." She tried to steer Courtney away.

"No, wait," Courtney protested, not taking her eyes off Winnie. "Be sure to let us know if there's anything we can do to help. The Tri Betas are committed to helping others in the community."

KC glared at Winnie, then at Courtney.

"Will do. Thanks," Winnie said cheerfully, turning to continue her jog down the sidewalk. Her face turned serious for a moment. "Amazing how scary the world can be sometimes, isn't it? Makes me glad I'm married now." Winnie clamped her headset back over her spikes and resumed her grin. "Catch you later," she yelled over her shoulder.

KC watched Winnie's retreating figure with a clenched jaw. She feared the worst had just happened.

Courtney was staring too. "You know, Winnie's funny hair and clothes used to grate on my nerves. But no more. I'm really glad we ran into her."

"Really. Why?" KC asked anxiously.

Courtney looked directly at KC. "I know you mean well, KC," she began, touching KC's arm. "I was about to approve the gazebo. Maybe the Tri Betas do need a little psychological boost."

KC nodded vigorously. "They do."

"But there's no turning back now," Courtney went on. "We're not a sorority that squanders precious funds on our own pleasure while people starve and die of terrible diseases."

"But we do care!" KC shouted.

Courtney shook her head. "Caring means *no* gazebo," she declared. "That's my decision."

KC sighed. Trouble within the sorority was just beginning.

Five

"So anyway," the *Weekly Journal* editor, Greg Sukamaki, was droning on, "we'd practically put the paper to bed when Betty Archdale comes up to me and says she'd mixed up her facts on our front-page story. It turns out that old Mr. Whitehead from the Board of Regents didn't actually *die*. He was being *memorialized* by the state in the form of a freeway overpass on the interstate. She'd actually written an obituary on the guy—and we had to rip it out. . . ."

Dash closed his eyes and tried to shut Greg out. He knew his editor was just trying to get him up to speed since he got out of jail. But his desktop was now a small mountain of unreturned messages, half-written stories, and overflowing research files.

"Bummer," Dash muttered, realizing that he was too worried and agitated to work anyway.

"Hey, I'll stop talking." Greg put a reassuring hand on Dash's shoulder. "I know you've got a lot of stuff coming down. Any news from the cops?"

Dash gritted his teeth. "None. Except that they've got me on a short leash."

"It's crazy," Greg lashed out, planting one foot forward and crossing his arms. "You have no record. You're a big-time achiever type around campus. And your dad has big-time status and bucks. That alone usually works."

Dash gave him a bitter smile. "Maybe they didn't like the name *Ramirez*."

Greg chewed thoughtfully at his pencil eraser. "What are the police actually doing?"

Swiveling around in his desk chair, Dash absently played with his dead computer keyboard. "Who knows? They don't answer my phone calls. They've pegged me as the 'punk with the Molotov cocktail.'"

"Even though you were just trying to get the bomb safely out of the building?" Greg shook his head in amazement.

"Are you kidding?" Dash shouted, throwing his pencil. It whistled and spun across the newsroom, causing several staffers to look up. "Once those ODT frat boys saw me running out of the smoking building with the bomb in my hand, something clicked in their underworked, Neanderthal brains. *Ah-hah! It's him!*"

"Scumbags."

"Then the cops arrived on the scene," Dash continued, crossing his arms and squeezing them against his chest. "And who do you think they believed? A bunch of blond frat boys in pressed chinos and button-downs—or me? Me—looking like a madman with dirt and blood all over my face?"

Greg nodded. "That's right. You said the skinheads worked you over pretty bad when you were following them that night."

"Right." Dash nodded fiercely. "So the cops decided I made up the story about Billy Jones and his friends with the shaved heads and the swastika tattoos."

"Made it up," Greg repeated, shaking his head. "You're in one hell of a jam, buddy."

"You're telling me?" Dash slammed his elbows down on his desk. "The cops think the Nazis went out of style after World War Two. They can't believe they're back. They won't even look—especially not in Springfield. It's too nice a place."

"Man," Greg breathed before heading back to his desk. "Get a good lawyer."

Dash held his head between his two hands and dug his fingers into his hair. He could feel the old fury building up inside him again—a long, slow boil that never went away. It had been there with him, just below the surface, every day and every night ever since he first laid eyes on the swastikas and the messages of hate.

He rubbed his neck, restless. Youth for a Pure America, he thought back with disgust. It wasn't just that the thugs had threatened him and beaten him up for being Latino. They were threatening anyone and everyone whose skin tone wasn't lily-white. They'd scrawled racial insults all over U of S Multicultural Week posters and flyers. They'd taunted and chased his friend Abraham Allen, who was black. Then they'd plotted to firebomb the Tri Beta house after they learned the sorority was hosting the black inner-city poet Rico Santoya.

Dash straightened up and took a gulp of cold coffee. He couldn't get the sick, ugly neo-Nazi faces out of his head. The fact that they were still running loose made his blood run cold enough. But the fact that the ODT frat brothers, the police, and nearly everyone else thought he'd actually firebombed the Tri Betas, well . . . He sprang to his feet and stuffed his hands into his jeans. It was just too crazy for him to believe.

Dash spun around, heading for the coffee machine. Then he stopped. Bursting through the newsroom door was Lauren, her wispy hair flying and her wire-rimmed glasses slipping down her nose.

Dash sat down again and watched her approach. Wearing her familiar oversize denim jacket over a thrift-store skirt and high-top sneakers, she looked like her usual intense self. But today she looked even better than usual. Dash propped the side of his face up with his elbow, staring at her. Maybe it was because she was the one person he knew absolutely believed in his story.

The one person who'd go out on a limb for him.

The one person he loved.

Dash nodded at her as she approached. Lauren had guts, integrity, and courage. He didn't really understand what had gone wrong with their relationship. But there was only one thing he longed for more than his freedom.

And that was Lauren.

"Hi," Lauren said, flopping down on the scraggly, overstuffed chair next to his desk. Her iridescent violet eyes looked desolate. "Don't mind me. I'm just on my way to *West Coast Woman,* trying to decide whether to write 'How to Cut Out the Fat—Western Style' or 'Organize Your Desk—Organize Your Life.'"

Dash gazed at the smooth white skin of Lauren's neck. "Don't sweat it," he said gruffly, leaning back in his chair. "The powers-that-be just want you to pay your dues. Once they see you've got talent, they'll work you to the bone."

"The *power,*" Lauren snapped, "happens to be a man. The power*less* magazine staff happens to be all women. Sound familiar?"

Dash lifted a corner of his upper lip in disgust. "Yeah. It sounds familiar. It sounds unfair. And life is unfair, kiddo."

"Oh, shut up," Lauren snapped. "I come in

here. I sit down next to you. I tell you my problem. And you blow me off."

Dash shrugged, wondering why things always got turned around with Lauren. Why were they arguing? Why couldn't they just fall into each other's arms and take care of each other forever? "You have to work with a man. You have to write one fluff piece. It just doesn't seem like that big a deal, Lauren. I'm sorry."

Lauren was staring at him as if she were thinking hard about what he'd just said. Then he could see her chest heave as her head flopped back on the couch. "I hate this."

"I know."

"And I'm sorry to unload on you. You have more important things to think about."

A warm feeling slipped through Dash. Maybe it was hope. Maybe it was just the comforting sound of Lauren's voice when she wasn't angry. "No, no," Dash flipped back. "Actually, I'd rather think about fluff pieces for a while. It keeps me from thinking about all the jail time I'm in for. I need an escape."

A slow, sad smile sneaked out of the corner of Lauren's mouth. "Okay."

Dash leaned forward and fiddled shyly with the arm of the couch where she sat. His eyes locked on Lauren's. "I've got to get out of here. Let me walk you down to the magazine. Maybe I can help you decide which airhead idea fits you best."

Lauren bit her lip. "Okay," she said cautiously.

"As long as you don't go into the magazine office with me and start ladling out advice to the staff."

"Never."

"Right," Lauren shot back, heading out the newsroom door, looping her bag higher up on her shoulder and tossing a soda can in the recycle barrel on her way out. "You know you want to."

Dash let himself laugh. "So what if I do? I can control myself."

Once they were outside, Dash breathed a little easier. The mountain air was crisp, and his dark thoughts of white supremacists and prison time suddenly faded. Skaters zoomed by. Couples on the front grass held hands. The smell of frying hamburgers wafted under their noses. Nothing had really changed. At least for now.

As they approached downtown Springfield, the air got grittier, and the sound of honking horns put Dash on edge. He stepped over a grate. Maybe it was because they were near the city jail, where he'd been locked up for two days, unable to sleep.

"Okay," Dash spoke up. "Story ideas. How about 'Ten Steps to a Younger You?'"

Lauren giggled and nudged him in the side. "'Ten Steps to a Cleaner Closet.'"

"'Ten Steps to a Cool Boyfriend.'"

"Ha!" Lauren burst out. "Like you, for instance?"

Dash looked down at his boots, hurt. There was a definite change in Lauren. She was tougher, more independent. It was pretty clear she didn't need him anymore. Why did he always want to believe they would find a way to connect? It just wasn't going to happen. She was too preoccupied with her own life.

"Hey, look," Lauren began, slipping her hand on his shoulder. "I didn't mean . . ."

Dash shrugged her hand off. "No. It's nothing."

"Come on, Dash," Lauren tried to soothe. "I was just fooling around."

"Well, don't fool," Dash said hotly, not looking at her.

To their right, he could see the city courthouse and the jail coming into view. He fingered his stubbly chin between his thumb and forefinger. As long as he was there, Dash thought, he might as well try to get a little information. He wasn't going to sit around passively while this investigation wallowed in the back of someone's file cabinet.

Dash stuffed his hands into his leather jacket and broke off from Lauren on the sidewalk. Hopping lightly up the grassy slope, he turned back to look at her briefly. "See you around. I'm going to check in with my friends at the city jail."

"I'm going with you," Lauren yelled, scrambling up the slope behind him. "You're too belligerent to face them alone. They're looking for a reason to get you, Dash. There's nothing they'd like better."

"Suit yourself," Dash muttered, hopping up the granite steps, his pulse quickening, his fury sloshing toward the surface. What was the problem? Why couldn't he just go to school and have Lauren and live a normal life like everyone else?

Jerking open the front double door, Dash stormed inside. His plan was to hunt down his arresting officer and see if he could get a little information.

"Hey, hey," said an officer in dark-blue pants and a light-blue short-sleeved shirt, grinning as he wrote something down on a pad. He was half leaning against the front desk in the reception area, his heavy stomach bulging over his black belt, and his dark-blond hair slicked back above his dark glasses.

Dash clenched his jaw. It was Officer Lyle Hearly, the cop he had first encountered after he'd stumbled out of the smoke-choked Tri Beta house.

"What's the matter?" Officer Hearly chuckled, slipping one muscular hip onto the edge of the desk and crossing his arms. He looked Dash up and down with contempt. "Can't stay away?"

"Why haven't you returned my phone calls?" Dash blazed, heading fearlessly toward him until they were practically nose to nose.

"Got nothing to say," Hearly replied calmly. "In fact, the case has been closed. As far as we can tell, little ol' Springfield doesn't have a skinhead to its name. I think those folks hang out where they can get a little more action, Ramirez."

"You're wrong!" Dash shouted. "I followed them for three days before they hit the Tri Beta house. I've told you where they hung out. I've provided you with descriptions. What more do you want?"

The officer glared back. "Nothing. Not a darn thing. We just want you to stay out of it. No amateur investigations. No adventures. No nothing. We don't want you anywhere except class, the library, and that neat little room you rent. Got it?"

"You don't know . . ." Dash began to yell, before he felt a warning hand on his shoulder. He sunk his head down and turned. Lauren was tilting her silky head toward the door.

"Lay low and stay out of this, kid," Hearly sneered. "Or we'll slam you back in here so fast your head will spin."

"Come on," Lauren murmured, grabbing him by the elbow and dragging him out the glass doors.

As soon as he was outside, Dash jerked away and zigzagged angrily across the lawn in front of the building until he threw himself into a bench on the noisy sidewalk. Lauren sat down next to him.

"You're right. They're useless," she groaned.

"They've got me, Lauren." Dash rubbed his hands up and down the tops of his jeans. "Do you see? If something doesn't break soon, I'm a dead man."

"Tell me what I can do to help." Lauren's eyes were planted on his face, deadly serious, as if nothing around them existed. "I'll do—anything."

Dash looked back at her in wonder, almost afraid to touch her. On the surface, she was soft—delicate. Inside, she was absolutely tough. Absolutely loyal. And absolutely committed to the truth. It was what made her such a great writer. It was why he loved her so much. "You'd do that for me?"

"Yes," Lauren said, barely moving her lips. Her violet eyes were wet, but the longer he looked into them the more he could see the fire inside.

"Thanks," Dash whispered, turning away from her so she couldn't see his face crumpling and his eyes hot with unfamiliar tears.

"Please . . ." Lauren gripped his upper arm and leaned over so that she was looking into his face. "Please don't give up."

Dash's chest heaved a couple of times. He gave in and began to cry, leaning his head onto her shoulder. She wrapped both arms around him, oblivious to the passersby on the busy sidewalk. "You—you want to help," Dash choked out the words, "and I don't even know what to tell you to do."

"We'll think of something, Dash," Lauren said softly. "We'll think of something."

Winnie gulped her herbal tea, sat up in her chair, and punched the telephone button for the fifteenth time that afternoon.

"Crisis Hotline," Winnie said calmly, poising her pencil over her notepad while fiddling playfully with the spiky nest of her hair.

"Hi," a young girl's soft voice came on. "Um, this is really embarrassing, but . . ."

"It's okay to be embarrassed," Winnie broke in gently. "What's important is that you called."

"Um, okay, but what I need to know is—well— you can't get AIDS—um—unless you're gay, right?"

"Wrong," Winnie said firmly. "Anyone can be exposed to the HIV virus by having sexual intercourse, or getting infected blood in your system, or by sharing IV drug needles. In fact, among young people like us, one in every eight AIDS cases originates with sexual contact between a girl and a guy."

"Oh."

"If you're worried, check in with the health center and get tested," Winnie reassured her. "Then you can either stay away from sex altogether— which is a perfectly sane and safe option in this day and age," Winnie ran on, "or you can play it absolutely safe, by using a condom every single time you have sex. And I mean *every* time. Don't put your life into someone else's hands. There are plenty of other sexually transmitted diseases out there you want to avoid too—not to mention an unwanted pregnancy. I'll send you a brochure for more info, okay?"

"Thanks. That'd be great."

"And don't fool around with drugs or alcohol if you're planning to have sex," Winnie warned. "There's no way you're going to remember all this if you're not thinking straight."

"Thanks again."

"No problemo," Winnie said confidently, scribbling down the girl's address. "And be sure to check out the AIDS danceathon coming up this weekend to raise money for the local AIDS hospice. It's going to be hot."

Winnie finally hung up the phone and put her red high-tops up on her desk.

"Imagine," she muttered proudly to herself. "Me—once the Queen of Danger and Outrageous Screwups—telling another person to play it safe. Me—formerly the-girl-with-a-new-rebel-boyfriend-per-week—a married woman with a baby on the way."

Winnie sighed with satisfaction, stood up, and stretched. It was four P.M. and the downtown Springfield Crisis Hotline center was quiet. In the next booth, she could hear Teresa Gray's soothing voice on the telephone. A door slammed in the distance. Winnie gazed at the dozens of photos and souvenirs that lined her tiny cubicle. Pictures of her husband, Josh Gaffey. Photos of Faith, KC, and Lauren mugging together on their trip to Hawaii.

At last, her life felt secure and happy. Even though she and Josh were only freshmen, their spontaneous marriage was working out. And even though the news of her unplanned pregnancy had practically driven them apart, something had made them stick together.

She glanced at her watch. Time for Josh to pick her up and take her home to the safe, warm house they shared together. Their refrigerator was filled halfway with food. They were acing all of their classes. And they hadn't been to a party in two weeks. So what if it sounded dull and conservative? They had a life.

"Ready to go?"

Winnie turned around and grinned. It was Josh. Dressed in his usual shredded jeans, bleach-stained T-shirt, and leather jacket, Josh had an anxious look on his face. "You bet," Winnie replied, jumping up to kiss him on the cheek and grab her purse.

"How'd it go?"

"Okay," Winnie replied, slipping her arm quietly through Josh's. She stared lovingly at the tiny blue earring he wore in his ear and the familiar woven band he wore around his wrist. Her life with Josh was safe, all right. And she was beginning to realize how much she liked it that way.

She wanted her baby to be safe too. She couldn't resist looking down briefly at the small roundness of her stomach. Eleven weeks along. The tiny fetus underneath was about two or three inches long now. Its organs were developing and blood was flowing through its microscopic veins. It was hers. Hers and Josh's.

"Bye, Teresa," Winnie called out just before she slipped out the front door with Josh, past the cheerful pots of red geraniums lining the path.

"I brought the bike," Josh said casually, striding over to the shiny motorcycle parked next to the curb.

"Oh."

Josh slung his leg over the seat and handed her a helmet.

"Thanks," Winnie said, taking it slowly. For a moment, she just stood there, looking at Josh's familiar, quirky face, wondering what everything would be like after the baby was born. What he'd be like. How their life would change. She wanted everything to be perfect.

"Come on, Win," Josh urged her, bouncing the seat a little. He jammed on the engine and the quiet neighborhood was suddenly filled with its startling roar.

Winnie stiffened, then she walked closer to him and touched the sleeve of his jacket, her fingers running down the leather as if she'd never felt it before.

"Win?" Josh looked back, revving the engine. "Let's go."

Winnie lifted her lips to his ear. "We could have walked. It's a nice afternoon."

Josh shook his head irritably, then shut off the engine. "What's wrong, Win?"

"I'm pregnant, Josh—and the bike is dangerous," Winnie said simply.

Josh sighed. "Look, can we talk about this at home? It's been a long day."

Winnie slipped reluctantly onto the seat and began buckling her helmet on. "What are we going to do after the baby is born, Josh? Strap it onto the back wheel? It's just not going to work."

"What are you saying?"

Winnie wrapped her arms around Josh's waist

and positioned her feet. "I'm saying that we'll need a big, safe car."

"Big, safe family cars are expensive, Win." Josh adjusted himself in the seat so that he could look back at her. "Our baby's going to be safe, but I for one am not going to turn myself into a suburban automaton who slaves to make payments on his minivan."

"Automaton?" Winnie came back slowly, feeling the heat rise inside of her.

"Yes," Josh insisted, turning away and flipping his hair back as he gripped the wide-spaced handlebars. "As in a person with no imagination or life? Who thinks only of the money he needs?"

Winnie hugged Josh closer, trying to control herself. This was no time to get into an argument. "I'm not asking for an automaton—or a minivan, Mr. Data. And I don't have all the nitty-gritty details about car prices and loans. All I know is that we have to find a safe car, and pronto."

Josh was silent as he turned the key in the ignition. Winnie tried to lean around his narrow back so that she could give him a big smile. But as she did, Josh suddenly flipped down the kickstand, stepped on the gas, and roared out onto the street.

"Josh!" Winnie gasped, struggling to straighten up on the seat.

But Josh didn't answer. All Winnie could see was his silent back as they swerved sharply around a corner and sped toward home.

Six

"**W**e needed it yesterday," a *West Coast Woman* editor was barking over the phone as Lauren stormed down the magazine office's carpeted hallway.

Lauren had just left Dash near the front entrance of the Springfield courthouse and jail. The inside of her head was like a television set that kept flipping from station to station. The horrible, flashing images were out of her control.

The mocking look on Officer Hearly's lumpish face.

Dash—the one who was always so sure of everything, crumpled on her shoulder, crying.

The steel bars on the prison cell.

Lauren clutched the strap on her shoulder, trying to steady herself. Before this afternoon, she hadn't realized how serious Dash's situation was. If the police didn't get something on the local skinhead gang—and soon—Dash could be facing serious charges. Charges that would cost him years in jail.

"I've got to get that disk back," another woman was yelling across the open-air office. "It's my only copy."

"Daria?" someone else was shrieking sarcastically. "Did you proof page twenty, or is 'potato' really spelled with an 'e' on the end?"

The hairs on Lauren's back stood on end. What were they getting so worked up about, anyway? The *West Coast Woman*'s office suite was tasteful enough. And its coffee smelled as if it had been rushed from the yuppiest roaster in town. But its atmosphere was about as mature as a daycare center's.

"Just get it to me fast," Jamie was snapping into the telephone as Lauren entered his sleek office. His irritable voice made Lauren's mood go from worried to black. Earlier that day, he'd called and asked her to come down to discuss the article she'd be writing for the magazine. Now all she wanted to do was throw his story-idea list in his face and leave *West Coast Woman* forever. But by this time, he was nodding to her eagerly, motioning for her to sit down.

Lauren sat down stiffly, not taking her purse off her shoulder. She stared blankly at the framed cartoons and political caricatures hung neatly on the wall.

"No way," Jamie was growling into the receiver. He stuck a finger under his dress-shirt collar and worked it loose, rolling his eyes up to the ceiling. "Look, Marsha. Don't make it a diet piece. That's all I'm asking. Women are sick of diets. They want to hear about fitness and clothes that make them *look* thin. Forget the diet." He slammed down the phone and looked up. "Just a moment." He picked up the phone again and punched a button. "Yeah? Oh, yeah. Sure. No, the shot of the cute baby in the briefcase did *not* work out. The nose is running. There's a sticky-looking hair. Yeah. Major touch-up time."

Lauren rolled her eyes. The entire world was going to hell, and *West Coast Woman* was having a stroke over diet articles and baby pictures. Some of her best friends were being firebombed out of their house. Dangerous skinheads were roaming Springfield. And Dash could be looking at a life behind bars. What was she doing here, anyway?

"Okay," Jamie blurted, slamming down the phone again and looking up. "Sorry."

Lauren stared at his uptight expression. His lips were pressed together and his small, intense eyes were darting about the room, as if he were still pondering his phone conversation. Then he took a deep breath, leaned back in his chair, and looked at her.

Lauren looked down at her lap.

"Lauren?" Jamie tilted his head to the side.

Lauren couldn't speak at first. She felt pinpricks of red-hot anger all over her body. The only question was, when would they burst into a nuclear explosion before she managed to get out of his stuffy office? "Uh, hi—uh—Mr. Wells."

"Jamie," he said quickly. "Just call me Jamie."

Lauren cleared her throat and looked away.

"Uh, well, have you picked your topic?" Jamie wanted to know.

Lauren wavered, wondering what to do, still sick at heart over Dash. Did she really want to write a fluff piece? Would it be worth it to get a shot at a national publication? "Not exactly," she answered softly.

"I see," Jamie said carefully, twisting the elastic band on his wristwatch. He bit the side of his lower lip thoughtfully. "Well—what did you think of the 'organizing your life' topic? Does that—uh—work for you?"

"Actually, I'm not very organized," Lauren said bluntly, giving him a challenging look.

"Okay." Jamie twisted his watchband again, then let it snap back in place. He leaned back in his chair and rocked it a little.

"Why don't you pick one?" Lauren finally said, wondering if he could hear the furious throbbing in her neck veins.

"Well, I thought—"

Lauren stood up abruptly. "I'm sorry, I shouldn't have come."

Jamie's mouth dropped open.

"It's just that I—uh—" Lauren continued, desperately thinking of an excuse that would get her out of the sterile office and back into the real world where she could do some good. "I don't think I can do the work."

"Lauren, that's crazy." Jamie stood up, confused. "I guess I just don't understand what's happening here."

"I'll tell you what's happening," Lauren heard herself cry out. "There are some terrible things going on in this town that are worth writing about. And you people are spending your time and your space on sappy, irrelevant articles that are an insult to the women you pretend to want to read your publication."

Jamie's blue eyes seemed to draw back inside his head. He stopped, then slipped his hip onto the side of his desk. To Lauren's surprise, instead of being angry, Jamie looked almost hurt.

"I'm sorry, Jamie," Lauren continued to smoke, "but I'm not interested in doing your grunt work. I know I'm only eighteen and a mere unpaid intern on this magazine, but there are stories in this town I *know* how to cover because I've done it before—with a lot of success."

"Well, I think—"

"Do you realize," Lauren barged ahead, cutting Jamie off, "that in the last week, the University of Springfield has been terrorized by a gang of skinheads who taunt and threaten anyone who's not white?"

Jamie stared.

"Do you realize that while you folks are in here writing about easy-gardening tips and yummy casserole creations, there are dozens of women in town who are now homeless? All because of a ruthless gang of thugs who firebombed their house and nearly killed all of them?"

For a moment, Jamie's office was completely silent. Then, exhausted and confused, Lauren sat back down, breathing hard, staring at the carpet, unable to say anything more. She felt drained, sad, and completely foolish. The only thing left for her to do now was crawl back to campus and try to salvage what was left of her pitiful career. First, though, she readied herself to hear Jamie's harsh response to her tirade.

But to her surprise, Jamie wasn't firing her. He wasn't glaring at her. In fact, he wasn't doing anything at all. She watched, almost afraid, as he sat frozen on the edge of the desk. His hands were slipped into the pockets of his dress slacks, but the sinewy muscles in his forearms were twitching and flexing.

Something clutched inside of Lauren's throat.

Slowly, Jamie stood up. He walked around his desk and stood quietly in front of a picture, his arms crossed. Then he sat back down in his chair and folded his hands in front of him. His head was bent, but his eyes were traveling up to her face as though he were a little boy about to make a confession to the school principal.

"You're right, you know," Jamie said.

Lauren's mouth dropped open. It was as if someone had opened a window. "I am?"

Slowly, Jamie's fist balled up. He smashed it down on his desk. "*Why* didn't you walk into this room a year ago?" He stood up and extended his hand. "Look, let's start over."

Slowly, Lauren put out her hand, bracing herself for another knuckle-smashing experience.

But this time, he took her hand gently.

"Shake on what?" Lauren replied, confused.

Jamie shrugged and smoothed down his pin-striped shirt. He sat back in his chair and bounced it up and down, staring at the ceiling, as if he were trying to put his thoughts into words.

"We market this rag as the toughest thing since beef jerky, then fill it with the stuff all the other women's publications run. What we need are more hard-hitting local stories."

Lauren could barely breathe. "It's not like it would hurt your circulation or anything," she ventured. "I mean, women want to know about social problems that affect their communities."

"Yeah," Jamie said absently, staring at his philodendron plant. "Yeah, I know."

"You get a good cover story on something tough and real," Lauren continued, "and people will pick up on it."

Jamie was doodling something on a legal pad. "If I have to write one more story about skirt lengths or potted plants," he said tersely, "I'll lose my mind."

"Of course you will," Lauren immediately agreed. She stopped herself, suddenly embarrassed. After all, she barely knew this guy.

"So." Jamie raised one eyebrow imperceptibly, as if he were checking her reaction. "What next?"

Lauren paused, still in shock. "Um—what do you mean?"

"I mean on this neo-Nazi stuff," Jamie said. "What's your angle?"

"You—you're interested in that story idea?"

"Yeah," Jamie replied quietly. "Yeah, as a matter of fact, I am. I'd like to move on this story. And if we can put something together, how about a joint byline? Your name first, of course."

"Sure," Lauren replied, widening her eyes in amazement. She supposed she could have hammered him for wanting to share the byline. But the guy was totally without machismo. And after all, he probably had a lot more journalistic experience than she did.

In fact, Lauren realized, he was probably handing her the chance of a lifetime. Not only was it the story *she* needed.

It was the story Dash needed.

Fund-raisers never come together easily, Faith thought as she waited for the Colin's House fund-raiser meeting to begin. There were always hitches. Screwups. Disagreements. But this one was different. Faith sensed magic in the room. People really seemed to care. This time everything fit together like a precision puzzle. Since Merideth had held the first meeting on the danceathon yesterday, more than fifty volunteers had signed up. All of

Faith's friends had been eager to help. And a hip, underage disco in downtown Springfield called The Glass Slipper had agreed to hold the danceathon for free—as long as they could do it this Saturday.

After all the ups and downs of her freshman year, Faith felt as if she had finally found a balance in her life. Not only was she in the Professional Theater Program. Not only was she out of a stifling relationship with her ex-boyfriend, Becker Cain. She finally had a cause to focus her life again. It was good to feel useful.

The door opened and Merideth ambled in, his hands shoved into the pockets of his black pants, his back slightly hunched. There was something in his vague, worried expression that made Faith frown. Even his usually ruddy face looked pale.

"Hi." Faith patted the seat next to her, facing the gathering group of volunteers.

"Hey," Merideth said hurriedly, sitting down and dumping his leather bag on the floor. His forehead looked sweaty and there were slight shadows under his eyes. "Are we going to pull this off?"

Faith nudged him in the side and gave him a reassuring smile. "I *know* we are. I can feel it in my mood ring."

Merideth's brown eyes were still dark. "Are we still without posters?"

"Are you kidding?" Faith flipped back her long braid and pointed to someone in the crowd. "That happens to be Danny Markam—the hottest cartoon-ist on campus. He made up the poster design last night. It's perfect. And if you like it, he's going to have copies made tomorrow morning. So they'll be up late tomorrow afternoon."

"Good." Merideth looked a little relieved. "I'd like to make a few grand on this thing. Colin's House needs the money so badly, Faith."

"Relax," Faith whispered as her friends Liza Ruff and Kimberly Dayton burst through a back door. Liza's bright-red hair looked as offbeat as her com-edy act, and Kimberly's lithe dancer's body seemed to tower gracefully over nearly everyone in the room. "Everything's going to be fine."

Merideth finally stood up. "Can we get started?" he called out. There was a rumbling of folding chairs. He had to stop his introduction when a huge group arrived, everyone chattering at once.

Faith was just about to turn her attention to Merideth when she saw someone familiar slip in the back and quietly sit down—someone who made her realize just how universal the AIDS problem had be-come.

It was Courtney.

An AIDS fund-raiser wasn't exactly the kind of project Faith imagined prim, conservative Courtney would be interested in. But then Courtney, she knew, wasn't your average sorority president.

The night before, over a study pizza at Winnie's place, KC had told her about the current feud over

Faith looked in wonder at Merideth. He was usually such a happy-go-lucky cutup. She'd never seen him so committed, so serious. And he'd never before mentioned a word about being an AIDS volunteer.

A guy Faith recognized from her western civ class was nodding in the second row. "My brother died of AIDS last year," he said quietly. "He was in a hospice that had a homelike setting and a comfort-care approach. But it was so isolating for him. Everyone I knew seemed to think they could catch the disease just by going there. His last few weeks were very lonely."

Merideth nodded, his eyes sympathetic. "It's an incurable disease, but the HIV virus that causes it is really pretty fragile. You can't catch it through casual contact, like a handshake or a shared telephone receiver."

A murmur of recognition rippled through the room, and a group of graduate students from the history department began talking among themselves.

Finally, Merideth held up a hand for quiet. "One more announcement before we go. The health center is offering free HIV tests for the next couple of weeks. That's the virus that causes the AIDS disease, as you probably already know. I'd encourage anyone who has been sexually active or used IV drugs to be tested."

Faith swallowed. The room was suddenly silent.

"Hey." Merideth tried to sound casual, though Faith detected a catch in his voice. "The point is— you've got to make sure you're not a carrier of the virus, so you don't unknowingly pass it on to someone else."

A murmur of agreement floated through the room. Faith shifted uneasily in her seat. For the first time, she began to wonder about her own past, though she'd had only one partner, Eliot Potter, a warm and lovable comedian she'd directed in a campus production. Looking back on it, the decision seemed so random, so unexplainable. She'd never thought much about AIDS, or the fact that unprotected sex was something that could literally kill you.

The whole mysterious puzzle made her shudder.

Why Eliot? Why not Brooks Baldwin, her high-school sweetheart? Faith suddenly thought. Why not Scott Sills, the easygoing volleyball player? Or Becker, the clingy philosophy major she'd roomed with for a week? She'd used a condom with Eliot. What if she'd gone ahead, unprotected, with someone else?

Faith gripped the edges of her folding chair, terrified.

Choosing a partner. Deciding whether or not to have sex. It wasn't something cold and clinical. It was pure, free, uncalculated emotion, right? It was chemistry. It was timing. It was real.

Maybe that's what made AIDS so terribly difficult to face, Faith thought. It was like a dark cloud that had swept over the whole experience of physical closeness. Spontaneity wasn't safe anymore. Knowledge and trust had to fit in now, somehow.

And that wasn't easy.

"I took the test myself a few days ago," Merideth said suddenly.

Faith broke away from her thoughts and looked over at him, stunned.

"And I should get the results back anytime now," he added, glancing nervously around the room.

A shiver ran through Faith, and her clipboard nearly slid off her jeans and onto the floor. She looked up in time to see Robert cast a nervous smile toward Merideth.

Then it hit her. *Of course Merideth got tested. He's high-risk. He needs to know.* All of her lighthearted excitement about dances and posters was completely gone now—sunk like a stone in a deep sea.

Merideth? Merideth could have the HIV virus? Of course he could. Anyone could, Faith thought as a wave of fear washed over her. AIDS wasn't something that happened to unfortunate people she didn't know. AIDS wasn't just a cause she was working on so that she could feel better about herself.

It was a disease that took lives. Maybe even the lives of the people she knew and loved best in the world.

Seven

Back at the Tri Beta house, a dozen girls were wearily dragging themselves into the kitchen after a three-hour-long wallpaper-peeling session in the foyer.

Surrounding them were drop cloths, ladders, and trash cans filled with charred debris.

"My nails are never going to be the same," complained a sophomore Tri Beta sister, scrubbing her hands irritably in the kitchen sink. She sighed and wiped them on a grubby dish towel.

KC rolled her eyes and looked down at her own raw hands and filthy jeans. Her hair was coming undone from its ponytail holder, and there was something scratchy and sharp in her sneaker.

All she wanted to do was take a shower back at the dorm and curl up with her western civ textbook.

"Courtney never showed up," Marcia Tabbert noted, whipping off her painting smock and stepping out of her boots. She ran her fingers tiredly through her freshly permed hair. "I can't believe it. *She* organized this cleanup session. Can't she bring herself to show up?"

Diane Woo nodded her head in agreement. A smudge of white plaster smeared her delicate nose. "It's the same old story. Courtney makes the rules, then she doesn't even follow them. All she does is check in on us—then run off to the nearest political cause. God, I'm sick of it."

"Courtney wants to save the world," another Tri Beta snapped, yanking open the refrigerator and pulling out a chilled bottle of imported spring water.

KC bristled. "Maybe Courtney is out visiting alumni, trying to get more donations."

"Right," Marcia tossed over her shoulder, trying to scrub white latex paint out of her nails. "But it's more likely she's out mingling with the poor and downtrodden tonight. And they definitely won't be writing any big checks for us."

"Courtney is great at raising funds, and you know it, Marcia," KC defended her. "She's a better persuader than any of us. Just the other day, old Mrs. Wiley personally sent her a check for three thousand dollars."

Diane turned around slowly from the sink, the

tap still running. "What?" she said in a weary monotone. "She did *what?*"

"Yes, didn't Courtney tell you? Mrs. Wiley said we could use the money any way we wanted to fix up the house. But she thought a backyard gazebo would be a fun project."

Suddenly, the kitchen was completely silent. Diane was staring at Marcia and KC was staring at both of them.

"AH," Marcia screeched, "I'm going to lose it. I'm going to absolutely lose it. Someone get me out of here. I need some *air*. I need some *food*. I need a *massage*. Courtney got three thousand dollars and didn't tell anyone?"

"Come on, Marcia," elegant Regina Charles spoke up, running a comb through her straight blond hair. "We're all tired. Let's talk about it later. Courtney can't keep us informed on every check she gets in the mail. She'll bring it up at the next Monday meeting."

"But I see Courtney every night at Mrs. Gomez's house," Diane sputtered. "She *always* used to share information about major donations like that. If she doesn't bring it up on Monday," she barked, "I expect you to, KC. You're the one who knows about the check. And you should be the one to force the issue—if you care anything about the future of this sorority."

KC was silent. A dozen pretty faces snarled. Diane's fists were clenched, and Marcia looked as if she was prepared to attack the next Doberman pinscher that walked through the door. The room had become so quiet that KC nearly jumped out of her skin when the refrigerator kicked on.

"Okay," KC finally said, lightly lifting her purse off a wall hook.

"Okay, what?" Diane's hand was jammed into her hip like a gun in a holster.

"Okay I'll *talk* to her," KC said through her clenched teeth. "Now I want to leave. Good-bye." KC stormed through the door, realizing in that moment what her Tri Beta sisters were doing. They knew she was close to Courtney, even though she was only a freshman. And now they wanted her to act as a go-between, to prove her loyalty to the whole group. KC knew she didn't have much choice.

It wasn't as if she didn't know where Courtney was coming from. For all of her life, KC's parents had been chasing after causes. They'd marched for bans on nuclear weapons. They'd raised money for the local soup kitchen, and practically gave away their own meager restaurant supplies trying to keep it alive. Her father had even chained himself to a redwood tree once, protesting a nearby timber yard.

"But Mom and Dad knew when to say no," KC whispered to herself, remembering her generous father. "They never neglected the people who really depended on them—like me and my brothers."

Courtney, on the other hand, did not have any experience with the poor and sick. She seemed to be running off as if she'd never seen anyone in need before.

Up ahead, KC could see the lights of Langston House and the usual tangle of chained-up bicycles and groups of students chattering around the front entrance. This time, however, she saw someone that made her heart beat slow and warm.

Slowing down and smoothing her hair back, KC didn't take her eyes off Cody. His long frame was sprawled casually on the wooden stairs, directly under a lamppost, and he was reading a thick paperback novel. She stepped closer, and as she drew near the shadow of his face, everything else gradually fell away. Courtney. The fire. Her snarling sorority sisters. Everything.

"Hi." KC stood in front of him, her arms at her sides, her breath quickening, her pulse roaring behind her ears like an ocean wave.

Cody looked up, drew in his long legs, and rested his arms on his knees. "Come here," he said quietly, his voice tender, his smile very white in the dim light. The sleeves on his plaid flannel shirt were rolled up, and KC stared down at the straight, clean muscle lines under his cinnamon skin.

KC sat down next to him and melted the side of her face into his shoulder. Then she slipped her hand down the inside of his arm and into his upturned fingers. Touching him made KC's skin prickle all over. She looked around. The dorm green was dark and quiet. She didn't see anything. She could feel only Cody's hand. She could smell only Cody's shirt. There was only Cody.

"Come on inside?" Cody whispered in her ear.

KC's heart was in her throat. She rose in a dream. "Sure."

"I need to study and I want company," Cody murmured, pressing his hip into KC's side as they strolled up the steps.

KC smiled, floating. "That's what I was hoping."

"I'm studying," Cody reminded her gently.

"Right," KC murmured back, climbing the stairs one heavy step at a time. It was strange. Her body was still aching from hours of wallpaper steaming, but her head now seemed perfectly clear and rested. She fingered Cody's soft collar, wondering what would happen the next moment. The next hour. The next year. Just being near Cody gave her a strange, restless feeling of anticipation that swept away everything in her mind except the fact that Cody was next to her.

"You worked hard today?" Cody slipped his chin onto the top of KC's head as she fumbled for her keys.

"Mmmm," KC mumbled. "I've been holding a twenty-five-pound wallpaper steamer for the last two hours. I want to forget about everything." She paused. "Wait."

"What?" Cody whispered.

"Annie."

"Oh, yeah."

"Annie's probably here," KC began, suddenly disoriented. "So let's, uh . . ."

Cody ducked down and pressed his lips against KC's bare neck. "Let's chill out a little?"

KC cleared her throat. "Uh. Yeah." She slipped the key into the door, coughed again, and opened it. It was dark inside. "Annie?" she said, flicking on the light.

"No one home," Cody said with a happy smile. He walked in and tossed his novel on KC's tiny bed. KC followed him, stepping carefully over Annie's suitcases and art-supply boxes piled neatly on the floor.

The bed squeaked loudly as Cody flopped down on it. He wedged the heel of one cowboy boot off with the toe of the other. The heavy boots dropped to the floor. "Ol' Maxey's killing us with another reading assignment."

"Oh?" KC teased, slipping onto the bed next to him and playing with his belt buckle. "Really?"

"I've got to get through *Hard Times* before Friday."

"You just finished nine hundred and fifty pages of *David Copperfield*!" KC exclaimed, propping herself up on one elbow and staring down at him with indignation.

She touched Cody's lips with a single finger, then bit his earlobe gently and whispered, "I think you should forget Maxey and Dickens."

"Uh-huh," Cody agreed, before he slipped one arm under her, sliding her over a little so that KC was on her back, looking up at his dark eyes. His face lowered and his mouth was on hers, first softly, then more deeply. Tiny shivers spread all over her body, as if someone were tickling her with feathers. Her arms slipped up around his neck, then down his back, until she was pulling up the bottom of his shirt with urgent tugs. She ran her hands up his bare skin, then held him with all the strength she had.

KC didn't know how much time had passed before she began hearing laughter. Music. Voices through the paper-thin walls. She shut her eyes tightly. She couldn't bear to have the moment end. But the noise was intruding.

KC rolled over abruptly, staring at her room's low, sloped ceiling. "Let's run away together."

"I'm for that," Cody answered back, stroking the hair off her forehead, smiling down. "When do we leave?"

KC stared at the shadows on the ceiling. "I like this dorm. And I like Annie. But I wish we could be by ourselves . . ." KC looked over at him shyly. "Sometime."

Cody's dark eyes were fixed on her. She watched him swallow, as if the idea made him almost nervous. "Your temporary roommate, I notice, is not here, darlin'."

KC sighed. "In a way I wish she were. She wasn't at the house tonight, and I want to talk to her about Courtney."

"Courtney," Cody repeated, releasing her.

"Yes, Courtney." KC gritted her teeth.

"KC?" Cody said gently. "Why don't we try to forget about the Tri Betas for a little bit? It's *you* I want to talk about, not Courtney."

KC covered her face with her hands. "You don't understand. The Tri Beta house is in ruins—and Courtney is off supporting every needy cause she can find in town. I'm getting dragged in because I'm Courtney's closest friend in the house."

For a few moments, Cody was completely silent as he lay on his side next to her. KC nestled close to him, listening to the rhythm of his heart, feeling the pull and take of his breath. In the dim light, she could make out the familiar gleam of the silver band he wore around his forearm. "I think Courtney knows what she's doing," Cody finally said. "She's growing up, KC. I bet her mama always told her to shoot for that slot at the top of the Tri Betas. And now that she's there, she's just high enough up the mountain to get a good look at the world. And it's not as pretty as she thought it was. What's wrong with trying to help?"

"Because she's neglecting commitments she's already made," KC snapped. "And anyway—since when are you on Courtney's side? Aren't you the same Cody Wainwright who was so suspicious when Courtney filed those sexual harassment charges last month?"

"Grrr," Cody growled playfully, tickling KC under her grubby workshirt.

"Stop!"

"Look, my pop had an old story that'll explain it," Cody began. "It's about two neighbors back in Hollow Grove, Tennessee, who were always quarreling about . . ."

KC slid on top of his outstretched body and clamped a hand over his mouth. "Cody?" she said sweetly. "Put a lid on it." Then, carefully, as she slid her hand away, she replaced it with her lips so that Cody had no chance to contradict her. Slowly, her hair fell forward like a curtain over their faces. His arms wrapped around her warmly and firmly. Their legs entwined, and KC gradually became aware that their two separate bodies had actually become one—his touch and hers seesawing back in an endless, blissful motion that KC never wanted to stop.

"KC," Cody whispered intently. "I want you, KC."

"Mmm," KC replied, floating on the lazy warmth of his kisses. "I want you, too."

"God," Cody murmured, kissing her forehead and moving sideways toward her ear.

KC caressed his face. There was something urgent now. Her head and body were spinning fast around her full heart. Everything in the room—in her life—in the world—had retreated into a distant mist. There was only one thing that mattered right now. Being as close as possible to Cody.

Then somewhere in a distant, foggy part of her brain, she heard a slight movement, but didn't pay attention. Cody was kissing her again and his hand was moving irresistibly around her bare waist.

"Uh—umm," someone cleared her throat.

This time, KC sat up abruptly, pushing her hair off her face. "What . . . ? Oh, Annie."

"I'm awfully sorry," Annie muttered. "This is really bad timing on my part. Oh, God."

"No, no." KC stared, not knowing what to say. Then she pulled her workshirt down as Cody struggled to sit up, tucking in his shirt. For a moment, all she could do was stare at Annie's fluffy red hair spilling over her shoulders. Her eyes were distraught and embarrassed and she still held her leather art portfolio in her hand, as if she hadn't decided whether to set it down and stay.

"Um, sorry," Annie said gently, scrunching up her mouth into an embarrassed smile. "I didn't realize . . ."

"Hey," Cody said good-naturedly, standing up. "Don't mind us. This is your room, not mine, after all."

Annie fiddled with one of her delicate earrings and looked away with a smile. "Look, I'll come back."

"Nope," Cody insisted. "Actually you came just in time. I was just about to lose my full professorship."

"What?" Annie said softly.

KC giggled. "Please come back, Annie. We didn't mean to . . . I mean we didn't know when you . . ."

Cody ducked down and gave KC a quick kiss. "Later, babe. I'm off to get a head start on tomorrow's radio show. Then I'll find a quiet corner for me and Charlie Dickens."

"Okay," KC whispered, watching his tall frame slip into the hallway.

"God, I feel terrible," Annie said, sinking down into the tiny cot. "I was in art class, but our live model got cold so we stopped early."

"It's okay. Really."

"I just don't want to ruin things for you. It's not my intention to squeeze out Cody," Annie said directly. "I can tell how strongly you feel about each other."

A smile crept out of the corner of KC's lips. Then she giggled. "Is it that obvious?"

"Yes," Annie blurted, joining her laughter. "Actually, it's more than obvious. It's like a freight train hitting you between the eyes. It's like wildfire. KC?" She began fanning her face with her hands. "Do you realize how hot this room is right now? It's positively steamy."

"Okay, okay. Stop!" KC protested.

Annie flopped back on the cot, clasped her hands together, and slipped them under her head. "I shouldn't tease, considering the couple of hot romances I've had. I'm the type to get a little carried away, I'm afraid. Whether it's a guy, or Picasso, or Mozart, or with my crazy fantasy about digging through a cellar in Rome and finding a lost Michelangelo."

"Nothing wrong with that," KC ventured. "Sometimes I wish I could be a little less uptight. I've always been so—I don't know, determined and . . ."

"Sensible?" Annie finished, sitting up and squeezing her knees together. "I think a little control isn't a bad thing. You can live a little *too* dangerously. Take last summer, for instance."

"What happened?" KC asked eagerly.

Annie rolled over to her side, her tiny silver earrings shaking against her ears. "I took an intensive art workshop in San Francisco and met this incredible guy from Italy who was a visiting expert on the restoration of sixteenth-century oils. He was older— about twenty-four—and had actually helped with the Sistine Chapel project."

"Amazing," KC breathed, her eyes widening. "What did he look like?"

"Dark, with a mustache," Annie began eagerly. "Big brown eyes. Tall. Built. And of course he drove a motorscooter."

"Of course." KC giggled.

"And of course," Annie held the back of her hand to her forehead in a mock faint, "he wore extremely dark sunglasses."

"Ooooh."

"We held hands. We walked across the Golden Gate Bridge. We ate a lot of Italian food, and it lasted a month," Annie summarized with a mischievous gleam in her eye. "I was breathless for thirty days."

"God," KC breathed, afraid to sound too innocent. After all, she hadn't ever slept with a guy. Not even Peter Dvorsky, her ex-boyfriend. She had loved him, but the right moment had never seemed to arrive. "So, what happened?"

"He went back to Italy!" Annie cried out crazily, throwing her pillow across the room. Then her face turned serious. "But now I look back on it and think I really shouldn't have . . . Well, you know what I mean."

"Yeah," KC answered, wishing she *did* know what Annie meant. How *had* Annie made that decision? When would she and Cody?

"But look, KC, if you need to have this room for the whole night—to be with Cody—just say the word," Annie continued casually, getting up and going to the window. She wound her hair up and pinned it. "There's a place in the art studio where I can hide out. I got a key for a special project and never returned it. It wouldn't kill me to sleep there once in a while."

KC turned over and rested her chin on her fists. She had to admit that Annie's unexpected offer was beginning to give her chills of excitement. But why? Up until a few days ago, she'd always had her room to herself. Cody could have slept here anytime they chose. What had held her back? Was it just that Annie was giving her permission?

"Think about it," Annie mumbled, yawning and twisting her hair on her head.

"I will," KC answered, holding back. It was hard for her to talk with someone as experienced as Annie about why she'd never slept with anyone. Maybe she didn't even know herself. Had she been afraid? She wasn't now. Was she unwilling to lose control? She wasn't now. Was it about self-respect and waiting for the right person to come along?

Someone like Cody?

KC stared at the little flowers on her pillow. It was Cody, wasn't it? He would be her first, wouldn't he? A small smile of wonder slipped onto her lips. He was the one she loved and trusted more than anyone. And she wanted to be close to him. Very close.

Smiling to herself, KC reached for her western civ textbook.

She was going to take Annie up on her offer.

Eight

"One empty bottle of cheap bourbon," Jamie murmured, shining his flashlight along the dining-room floor of Billy Jones's deserted house. "Whew. This isn't like any other *West Coast Woman* story I've ever covered." He picked a can up off the floor and looked into it. "One greasy tuna-fish can filled with cigarette butts."

Scraaaaaatch.

Lauren froze and dropped to her knees behind an overturned vinyl chair. "Shhhh. Cut the light. What was that?"

"What?" Jamie whispered back, ducking down below a window.

Lauren crept along the grimy floor and peered out into the rutted side driveway. A few scraggly trees scraped against the window in the wind. She dropped her shoulders in anxious relief. "Sorry. I thought I heard something."

"Better safe than sorry," Jamie whistled, crawling into the filthy kitchen, which reeked of sour milk, musty rags, and urine.

For the past few minutes, Lauren and Jamie had been rummaging through Billy Jones's former Olive Street skinhead hangout, a crummy one-story house at the end of a dead-end street on the edge of town. It had been completely deserted, and after trying several old doors, she and Jamie had finally managed to open the back entrance.

"I don't think these guys have been around for a while," Jamie went on. "And I understand why. This place is a pigsty."

Earlier that day, Lauren had contacted Dash about the story they were planning for *West Coast Woman*, and he had eagerly told her every detail he'd turned up on Jones's neo-Nazi skinhead gang, including their address. Just before the Tri Beta fire, Dash had managed to spy on them through the bare windows of this very house. He'd turned up a lot of information—all of which was ignored by the police.

Lauren nodded, crawling away from Jamie. "It's just that Dash has warned me about these guys. They're dangerous. They carry guns. And they wouldn't hesitate to kill us if they knew what we were up to."

Jamie gave her a reassuring nod from across the dark room. "Let's just find what we need and get the hell out of here."

Lauren sat up on her knees and shone the flashlight along the shelves of an empty bookcase. All they needed was some evidence, and Dash said this place had been stuffed with it. Posters of Adolf Hitler and the Ku Klux Klan. Nazi marching music. Gasoline bombs. Ammunition shells. They were bound to find something.

Lauren crawled into a musty-smelling closet. They *had* to find something. Dash's whole life depended on it. If she could direct the police to some solid piece of evidence, she was sure they'd begin believing Dash's story.

"Dash said the skinheads' emblem was a snake with a knife in its mouth," Lauren said.

"Nothing in here," Jamie's voice came back from the kitchen.

"Check the cigarette brand in the ashtray," Lauren said lamely, beginning to wonder if they'd find anything that night. "It might come in handy."

"Camels."

"Uh-huh," Lauren tried to sound confident, turning over an empty shoe box, then backing out of the closet empty-handed. "See anything that says Youth for a Pure America?"

"No," Jamie called over his shoulder, crawling

into the living room and beginning to rummage under a collapsing sofa.

Lauren glanced over at him. His expensive office clothes were now gritty, and his forehead was covered with beads of sweat. She was starting to feel guilty for dragging him into this situation, but he'd been just as eager to explore the skinheads' former haunts, despite the danger.

Besides, Lauren thought, Jamie didn't really have to come. His part of the research involved contacting police in other midsized western towns, looking for other hate-gang problems. Their plan was to write about how the gangs breed fear.

"Nothing in here," Jamie whispered loudly, lowering his flashlight and crawling over to her.

Lauren ran her flashlight beam into a final room, a bedroom littered with week-old garbage, empty beer cans, and overturned chairs. "These guys are pros," she said over her shoulder. "They took everything. No gasoline cans. No trace of an emblem. Nothing."

"Wait," Jamie said softly, getting down on his hands and knees under the bed's stained mattress. "Oh, it's just a torn-out newspaper article on baseball."

He stood up and knocked the dust off his pants. "They may be full of hate—but they're not stupid. Come on, no one's watching. Let's just get out of here."

Lauren flicked off her flashlight, breathing hard.

"Come on." Jamie reached out his hand.

"This isn't working," Lauren snapped. It was crazy. She knew this dangerous gang of bigots was out there somewhere. But right now, they were like ghosts.

"It just means we're back to square one," Jamie said quietly. He led the way out to his van, which was parked down the alley.

Lauren got in silently and buckled her seat belt. Inside, she felt foolish. Here she was, an eighteen-year-old unpaid intern on a prestigious magazine, convincing its editor to follow her on a wild-goose chase. She knew what Jamie's silence meant as they drove off. She had wasted his precious time.

"Let's stop in here," Jamie said several blocks later. He pointed to a brightly lit coffee shop on Springfield's main drag. His eyes darted up and down the street as he searched for a parking spot, and the van slipped in neatly in front of the restaurant.

Lauren pulled her beret down on her head and got out. Then she obediently followed him to the restaurant, even allowing him to open the door for her.

"So," Jamie began briskly, once they were seated. He opened a huge, orange plastic menu and looked at it. "What will you have?"

Lauren lifted her menu and scanned it miserably. The trip to the so-called gang hideout was a complete flop. She knew Jamie suspected her of being some kind of whacked-out, would-be Nancy Drew. She knew he was just taking her out so he could let her down easily. All she had to do now was brace herself for a condescending explanation of why they had to drop the story.

"What can I get you folks tonight?" asked a waitress with a jet-black bubble hairdo.

"Well." Jamie slapped his menu down with enthusiasm and looked up at the woman. "We're celebrating tonight, so why don't you bring me the deluxe everything-in-it omelet with extra cheese?"

Lauren stared.

"Lauren?"

"Um. A cup of clam chowder and a small green salad," Lauren said blankly, looking at Jamie in confusion.

Jamie whipped a notebook out of his jacket, as if he remembered something. He flipped open the cover and stared intently at his notes. "We'll go back and interview the neighbors. They're bound to know something," he mumbled.

"You mean you want to stick with the story?" Lauren asked, looking up from her coffee.

"Of course!" Jamie said, setting his notebook down and looking up at her with his intense blue eyes. "Is there something wrong?"

"Well," Lauren mumbled, "it's just that we haven't found anything."

"We just started!" Jamie blurted, laughing a little, flexing his hands around the coffee cup the waitress set down in front of him. His eyes were shining. "You don't know me, Lauren. I don't give up very easily. You should have seen me in journalism school. I'd get stuck on the damnedest stories and then wouldn't let go until someone threatened to flunk me."

"No." Lauren giggled.

"Oh, yeah." Jamie shrugged. "They called me The Mule. It was terrible."

Lauren smiled.

"But the point is, Lauren, that we can't give up. False leads are par for the course. We have to keep digging."

Lauren opened her mouth to say something, then closed it.

Jamie took another sip of coffee and tilted his head. "What?"

Lauren shifted. "It's just that—well . . . you're so different than you seemed when I first met you. I mean, you seemed so set on doing those fluff pieces. And you were so blunt."

"Oh—yeah." Jamie stared down, embarrassed.

"I guess I just want to say—thanks for having the guts to go with this story," Lauren said right out. "I hope you won't be sorry."

"I'm sure I won't be," Jamie came back. There was an awkward moment when he didn't seem to know what to say. "And—yeah . . . I know what you mean about how I come off like an army sergeant with ants in his pants."

Lauren smiled at him.

"Frankly, it's an act," he admitted. "People assume I'm some kind of wimp because I work for a women's magazine. So after a while, I think I started turning on the machismo to make up for it. But hey, I like magazine work—and I wanted to live in Springfield if I couldn't work at one of the top New York magazines. I like this job. And by the way—the publisher is a woman. I have no problem taking orders from her, thank you very much."

"Wow," Lauren teased, stabbing her salad with her fork. "You're so politically correct I can barely stand it."

"Oh, that's me." Jamie laughed back, digging into his omelet. "Plus, when I took this job, I thought I'd meet a lot of smart, single women."

Lauren tilted her head politely, not knowing exactly what to say. After all, Jamie was her boss. She couldn't exactly slap him on the back and wish him good luck.

Jamie's face dropped a little, and for a minute, he looked down at his fork. "But it hasn't worked out that way."

"Oh, well—um," Lauren stammered, looking nervously at the waitress refilling their coffee cups, "I'm sorry."

"Actually, I've never been tempted," Jamie said, fumbling with his tiny jam container.

"Oh."

"Until . . ." Jamie started, swallowing and looking into her eyes, "until you walked into my office."

Lauren stopped breathing. Her eyes were darting around the tabletop, but she couldn't seem to lift them up to his face. What was he talking about?

"I felt something for you the moment you

walked in, Lauren," Jamie said quietly. "I guess that's why I acted like such a blustery jerk and practically wrenched your hand off."

Lauren cleared her throat, flustered. She could feel the scarlet creeping up her cheeks and knew there was nothing she could do about it. What was she supposed to do? Thank him?

"I'm sorry, Lauren," she heard him say awkwardly. "I—uh—I just . . ."

For a moment, Lauren just sat there, looking at Jamie's half-eaten omelet, not knowing what to say. She knew that she was beginning to like Jamie, but why did he have to come out with this? She wasn't used to declarations from guys she didn't know. She wasn't used to declarations, period. Or guys either, for that matter.

Plus, Dash was back in her life now. Wasn't he?

Lauren turned to look out the window, avoiding Jamie's eyes—trying to think of a response. The main drag was busy with high-school kids cruising casually back and forth. U of S students speeding by on bikes, and motorcyclists gunning their engines. She stared absently into the distance, thinking about Dash and not about what she was looking at. Then her eyes slowly, cautiously settled themselves on something right across the street.

Something familiar. Something that fit a puzzle. Dash's puzzle.

"What?" Jamie spoke up. "What's wrong?"

"Rusty green wagon," Lauren murmured to

herself, bringing her eyes into focus.

Parked next to a gas pump directly across from them was a beat-up, rusty, four-door, American-made station wagon. Lauren narrowed her eyes, wondering why she was fixating on this ordinary heap of junk with the rust around the wheels and the bent antenna that looked as if it was about to fall off.

"What is it?" Jamie insisted. "Did I just blow it, Lauren? Maybe I shouldn't have said anything."

Lauren's hand suddenly gripped the side of the table. Several guys in Marine jackets and army boots were sauntering out of the gas station's repair shop. Their shaved heads and snarly looks were enough to make her heart beat.

But when they jumped into the car and made a screeching U-turn right in front of the coffee shop, Lauren saw the thing she'd been waiting for.

"Jamie," she cried, leaping up. "That car. The green station wagon. It—has one blue door!"

"What?" Jamie answered.

"Come on," Lauren practically shouted, digging a bill out of her purse and throwing it on the table. "Don't ask questions. Just get in the van. Fast!"

Jamie rushed out the door behind her as she looked up and down the street, then pointed at the van.

"The key. Get your key," Lauren shrieked. "It's Billy Jones. The car. Right there at the light."

"We're outta here," Jamie replied, balling up his fists and making a run for the van. "There's no way we're going to let them out of our sight."

Nine

....

Josh winced at the numbers on his computer screen that evening, then rapidly punched another series of keys.

Beep.

He slumped in his chair and nervously tapped one knee up and down. The second set of numbers looked even worse. He looked around the computer room he shared with Winnie and their housemates, Clifford Bronton and Rich Greenberg. Then he sighed. On the side wall, a large poster of Rich's marionette stared back at him. Its wooden tongue was sticking out.

"Same to you," Josh muttered to himself.

"Huh?" Winnie piped up. Sprawled out on the

carpeted floor, Winnie was busily coloring in letter-
ing for one of the Colin's House benefit posters.
Wearing Josh's old boxer shorts, a tank top, and a
pair of sparkly red socks, she looked more like a kid
playing dress-up than a mother-to-be.

"Nothing," Josh mumbled.

"Stop vibrating," Winnie complained cheerfully,
wiggling her toes. "Or I'll dip you in blue poster
paint. Actually, it's called Deep Lagoon . . ."

Josh tuned Winnie out as he narrowed his eyebrows and glared at his computer screen. The numbers for their family budget-to-be were not adding
up. And they never would.

After tuition, he and Winnie each have six hundred dollars a month, for a total of twelve hundred a
month. *Take away five hundred a month for rent.
Seventy-five for utilities and Winnie's long-distance
phone bill. Then four hundred for groceries and maybe
a hundred dollars for extras like pizza and the occa-
sional tank of gas for the motorcycle. That leaves a
hundred and twenty-five dollars for the baby.*

". . . at the student union. Don't you think?"
Winnie was saying.

Josh's eyes darted up from the screen. He turned
around and looked at her. But just as he did, he felt
a searing pain wrap around his head like a steel vise.
"What?" he mumbled. "What did you say?"

"Josh!" Winnie protested good-naturedly. "I said
I'm going to put these extra posters up inside the
bathroom stalls of the women's rooms at the stu-

dent union. And you can post some up above the urinals in the men's. Okay? The danceathon is only two days away, can you believe it?"

"Um. Yeah. No." Josh leaned forward and cradled his head in his hands.

"Josh?" Winnie asked, her voice softening. Slowly, she got up and tiptoed toward him. "What's wrong?"

"My head," Josh said. "It's throbbing."

"Oh, no," Winnie whispered, slipping a cool hand along his neck, then sliding it down his back. She carefully rubbed his muscles and gave his ear a little nibble with her lips. "Can I get you something?"

"Yeah," Josh groaned, unable to get up. "Two aspirins and maybe a wet rag."

"Gee, Josh," Winnie said in wonder. "You're usually so content when you're curled up in front of your computer. You look terrible."

Josh just shook his head. Winnie was right. He usually felt his most creative and relaxed in the gray-blue light of his computer screen. But this time, his program didn't involve a fantastic medieval computer game or a new way to analyze scientific data.

It involved money. Money that was so out of reach, it could have been on Saturn.

"Here," Winnie announced, returning with a glass of water, tablets, and a rag. "Like my mom used to say: all better."

Josh gulped the tablets, plastered his head with the cool cloth, and leaned back. "Yeah, well, unfortunately, it's not going to make it all better."

Winnie snaked her arms around his neck and down the front of his shirt. "Aw, come on, Josh," she cooed. "I know you're worried about becoming a father. But everything's going to be okay. It will all work out. Things always do."

Josh lifted his head and stared back at Winnie, who was smiling blissfully. Looking at her now, it was hard to believe she possessed a stratospheric IQ, could complete a *New York Times* crossword puzzle in less than thirty minutes, and was acing all of her classes. What was wrong with her? Didn't she realize what was going on?

They were having a baby in six months.

And a baby cost money. How would they stay in school and get money at the same time? And if they dropped out, how would they ever find the good jobs they'd need to support a child? What would happen to his dream of designing programs for a cutting-edge software company?

"Winnie," Josh began desperately, raking his fingers through his dark hair. "Winnie, look at me. I've been doing my homework. I've been checking out costs and taking a second look at our budget."

"That's wonderful!" Winnie said excitedly. "We *need* to know just where we stand when the baby's born."

Josh's heart sunk. "But don't you see, Win? Diapers will be fifty dollars a month. If we both stay in school, daycare will be at least three hundred, probably more. Baby clothes and equipment will run into the hundreds. A safe car will cost thousands. And that doesn't even count the doctor bills."

"Josh . . ."

"Even if we stay in this house share with Clifford and Rich, we still won't be able to make ends meet," Josh ranted, pressing the rag into the sockets of his eyes.

"Josh," Winnie tried again gently. She slipped one of her thighs up on the chair leg and continued rubbing his back in small, lazy circles. "People have been having babies since the beginning of time. And it's probably never been the absolutely perfect time for anyone. But the baby is coming. And we'll go on. People will help. I know Mom will pitch in with some baby clothes and some extra cash."

"We're not turning into charity cases," Josh snapped, anxiously twisting his tiny blue earring.

"We'll pay her back," Winnie murmured. "You have to understand, Josh. Having a child together is going to be the most wonderful, deeply fulfilling thing we've ever done. Just imagine, every cell in this child's body is half yours and half mine. It's a miracle."

Josh looked at Winnie's damp eyes, trying not to feel guilty. But he couldn't help the way he felt. He'd been happy and contented with his life the way it was. He loved the U of S. He was one of the top computer programming students. He had friends. A motorcycle he loved to ride. And most important, he had Winnie.

Now, Josh thought miserably, all because they had neglected to use birth control *one time*, everything was going to change. He didn't want to grow up this fast. Someday he'd be ready for a family with Winnie. But he wasn't ready now. Now all he could feel was his heart sinking like a lead weight to the bottom of the sea.

"It's almost like a spiritual awakening," Winnie began droning.

Josh stopped breathing. His scalp began to sweat and his pulse was throbbing in his sore temples. "Stop it, Winnie!" he cried out. "Maybe pregnancy has given *you* a spiritual high, but I'm still back here on earth and the view doesn't look too good from here."

Winnie drew back, a horrified look on her face.

"I—I don't know," Josh struggled. He swallowed hard and took a breath, unable to look at Winnie's wet brown eyes. "I have to be honest with you, Win. I feel like—like I'm being smothered . . ."

"Smothered?" Winnie peeped, backing up and sitting softly on the bed.

"Smothered in responsibility," Josh stumbled. "I have to do something. I have to *act*. We can't just keep telling ourselves everything will be okay. Because it's not going to be okay unless we're prepared."

Winnie was silent.

"There's only one solution," Josh suddenly said, standing up and walking over to the door. He paced back and crossed his arms over his chest. "I'm going to look for a job."

"A job?" Winnie gasped. "How will you have time to study?"

"I'll start looking tomorrow," Josh said quietly to the wall, before turning away and walking out of the room.

"And you're listening to K-R-U-S, stereo FM in Springfield. Hi, folks, Cody Wainwright here for another hour. I've got some lazy tunes and a few hair-raisin' tales for you this Thursday afternoon. So mix yourself up a pitcher of lemonade and settle back down. The fun is just starting."

KC had just walked in the door to the KRUS studio. As usual, the waiting room was littered with stacks of old newspapers, junk-food wrappers, and unopened mail filled with demo tapes and CDs record producers were eager to have played on campus radio stations.

Flopping down on the ripped Volkswagen van backseat that served as the station's waiting-room couch, KC settled her eyes on Cody behind the soundproof glass. His hands were moving expertly among a dozen dials and switches, and his face was still and calm as it hovered over the mike.

KC shivered.

Since the night before, when Annie had offered to stay in the art studio, KC had thought of nothing but Cody.

They would spend the whole night together soon. Why the time had come, she didn't know.

Where it would lead to, who knew? All KC did know was that she was ready.

"The U of S chapter of the National Merely Skin-Deep Organization is holding its annual humming championship this Sunday afternoon at two in the Forest Hall Quad," Cody continued, holding up a ragged piece of binder paper and squinting at it. "It's for real, folks. Winners take home donated paraphernalia, including a full-color poster displaying your favorite Star Trek characters in full Starship *Enterprise* regalia."

KC smiled. She was proud of Cody. Even though he was only a sophomore, his folksy, off-beat afternoon show had become a campus hit.

"On a serious note, folks," Cody continued, staring into the mike. "It's no coincidence that the HIV virus that causes AIDS is spreadin' like wildfire among young folks like us. Know why? It's 'cause we're not careful. We're just too wild and crazy, and yes, some of you are having sex with people you just don't know. Not to mention the needles and drugs and junk a few others are going to have to stay away from. Okay? You're takin' too many risks."

KC shifted uneasily in her seat.

"That's what the folks over at Colin's House are trying to tell us, everyone," Cody continued. "And that's why you are going to head on down to The Glass Slipper this Saturday night at eight o'clock for the classiest danceathon of your life. Colin's House is a hospice in Springfield for folks who have AIDS.

And the danceathon's gonna raise money for it. So I've got two more words to say to you. Be there."

The instant he finished the announcement, Cody pinched in a programmed set of music and went briefly off the air. KC rushed into the studio and lowered herself onto his lap.

"You again?" Cody said, an urgent edge to his voice as he hooked her around the waist with his arm. He kissed her on each side of her mouth, then strong and full on her lips, sending a fizzle through her body. Then he stroked a length of her dark hair off her face and looked directly into her eyes. KC felt dizzy.

"I love you," she said, ignoring the looks they were getting from technicians in the adjoining soundproof interview room.

"I love you more," Cody told her, running his fingers down the side of her face and then tracing the outline of her lips with the top of his forefinger. "You coming to the danceathon? My shift here lasts until nine o'clock tomorrow, but I'll be there right after."

KC leaned back in his arms so that her head was resting on his shoulder. She fingered the silver band on his arm, taking in the warmth of his body and the leathery smell of his vest. "I'm not sure . . ." she began absently, unable to get her mind off what she was about to propose. "Faith's really involved. She'll probably drag me down there, but . . ."

"Got another date?" Cody teased, moving his hand down her short skirt, then tickling the back of her bare knee.

"Cody! Of course not." She raised her head up and buried her face in his warm neck.

"Oh," Cody reacted, taking in a sharp breath. He leaned over her to adjust a volume level.

"Um." KC unburied her face. "I know that you're really busy this weekend with shows and an exam on Monday," she began carefully, buttoning and unbuttoning the top button on his white shirt. She could barely breathe.

"Oooh—you're right," Cody answered, clutching her hair playfully and tugging it slightly, so that her neck fell back a little and he was in position to kiss it.

KC's pulse was pounding. "But I just thought that—uh—sometime this next week you'd like to—spend the night over in my room."

"What about Annie?"

"She has a key to the art studio," KC whispered, nuzzling him. "She said she could stay there. You could be my roommate instead."

Cody's arm tightened around her waist. "I—I don't know what to say, KC. I'm happy. But I . . . ."

"What?" KC pushed away a little so she could see him better.

"Hey," Cody said earnestly. "What's happened, KC? Why are you ready to take this step?" He stroked her cheek with the back of his hand. "It's just that—well—I'm in love with you, and I don't want to mess things up. Things are too good."

"Cody," KC whispered, tears stinging her eyes.

"What if it's all about something else?" Cody

pleaded. "What if it's about escape? What if it turns out you were only trying to escape from all the nuttiness over at that sorority of yours?"

"Stop," KC whispered again, slipping her hand over his mouth. "I don't have any motive except that I want to be close to you, Cody. I love you."

Cody's eyes were fixed on hers.

KC took a deep breath. "I really do. I'm serious."

"I'm serious too."

Cody's arms tightened around her. She could feel his chest moving in and out, and for the first time, she felt connected—really connected—to another person.

What else mattered except her and Cody?

What else mattered except that soon they would be together?

Completely together.

Ten

....

auren crouched against a garbage can, peering up at Billy Jones's dimly lit apartment window across the alley. She'd been sitting that way for the last half hour, and her feet were beginning to lose their feeling.

"Lauren?" she heard Jamie's low voice a few yards behind her. She could hear footsteps crunching against gravel, then felt a knee brush hers as he stooped down. His eyes glinted in the moonlight and the faint, spicy smell of after-shave drifted briefly past her. "Any movement?"

She shook her head and shifted position. "No."

"Damn."

After spotting the skinhead gang outside the coffee shop the other night, Lauren and Jamie had frantically combed the downtown area for the rusty green car. At first they thought they'd lost them, but as they were retreating back to campus, Lauren saw the car glide into the parking lot of a sleazy Springfield tavern called Dog Bones. Two hours later, the beer-soaked skinheads stumbled out and Lauren and Jamie finally got what they'd been waiting for: a trail back to the neo-Nazis' latest hangout.

Lauren lowered herself down and stretched out her legs in the dirt. Then she fumbled through the pockets of her denim vest for the half-eaten candy bar she'd stuffed in there hours ago.

". . . butts outta here . . ." she heard a sharp voice through the window, followed by hollow, rumbling noises and high-pitched laughter. Lauren's blood began to thump in her throat.

Jamie balled up his fist. "We've had our eye on these lamebrains for nearly twenty-four hours now— and we still don't have anything."

Lauren nodded. "These guys are real do-nothings," she whispered. "Harassing blacks, Latinos, and the gay community must be their sole interest in life. Other than that, all they do is watch television, drink beer, and listen to heavy-metal music."

"We need something solid," Jamie whispered urgently. "Something that clearly connects them to the Tri Beta fire."

"SHHHH!" Lauren motioned for Jamie to get down. "Someone's coming out."

They both hunched down as the first guy emerged from the side of the building, his army boots thundering down the wooden stairs. From Dash's description, Lauren knew at once it was Billy. She narrowed her eyes. For all his tough-guy reputation, he looked strangely small. His head was shaved, but under the glare of the bare light bulb over the door, she could see that he was nearly bald anyway. Like the other skinheads behind him, he wore a Marines jacket, a flannel shirt, and baggy camouflage pants.

"Stay outta my way," Lauren heard Billy mutter as he casually grabbed the collar of another skinhead whose neck was tattooed with the head of a snake. He let out an offhanded, staccato laugh, and Lauren shuddered. His small yellow teeth were pointed. His face was pale and mean, as if he had a chip on his shoulder that wouldn't go away.

In a flash, Lauren knew she'd never let go of this story. These were the punks who had called Dash a spic and had beaten him up. Who had taunted blacks and claimed that only whites were fit to live in their vision of a "Pure America." Who worshipped Adolf Hitler—the man who destroyed millions of lives in World War II, stalking *his* vision of a "purified" Europe. These were the guys who had nearly killed her and her friends at the Tri Beta house.

And Dash was going to jail because of these vicious punks?

Lauren clenched her teeth. There was no way she was going to let that happen. Just no way.

Jamie and Lauren remained crouched in position on the dusty gravel behind the garbage cans. In the meantime, two of the skinheads had entered into a small fistfight next to the car over something Lauren couldn't quite hear. Billy's two other followers yanked open the back car doors and were flinging themselves into the ripped backseat. Behind the wheel of the car, Billy was jamming his foot onto the accelerator and revving it up as loudly as he could. Then he shoved a heavy-metal tape in his machine and turned up the volume.

"These are five ugly cats," Jamie said under his breath. "As soon as they're in the car and around the corner, run for the van. And be careful. Okay. NOW!"

Lauren dug one foot into the gravel and pushed off, scurrying as fast as she could across the back alley. Once she reached the van, she jumped in, crouching low, almost expecting to be shot at.

"Okay, fellas," Jamie panted, sliding in behind the wheel next to her, his eyes glued to the wind-shield. "Come on. Show us where you're going to play tonight."

Lauren's upper body swung to the left as Jamie steered sharply around the corner. Desperately, she locked her eyes onto the two back lights on Billy Jones's car. Her hair was flying and her heart quak-ing as they tore down the dank neighborhood street toward the downtown area. Then without warning, the car turned off down Springfield Highway.

Lauren leaned forward in her seat and frowned. "Where are they going?"

Jamie shook his head. "I just hope they're not leaving the state."

"Don't say such a thing. That would make things difficult."

"More like impossible."

Lauren bit her lip and stared ahead. "Nothing's impossible. We're going to follow these guys. We're going to get something on them. And the police are going to start taking this thing seriously."

"Look at that," Jamie said, looking straight ahead.

"Yahoo," Lauren muttered sarcastically, watching Billy Jones and his gang stick their bare fists out of the car as they gunned down the highway. It was a kind of angry salute to the night. It made Lauren sick inside. "Why don't they just give the 'heil Hitler' salute and let everyone see them for who they are?"

"We should be so lucky," Jamie answered, his eyes lighting up as he gripped the steering wheel. Up ahead, the skinheads' car slowed down and veered into the parking lot of Springfield's grungiest bowling alley, The HiTop.

"I don't believe this," Lauren said in wonder. "Bowling?"

"Sure," Jamie said with a grin as he pulled into the lot and parked far away from the green car. "Gotta do something to stay in shape when you're working hard to purify America."

"Right." Lauren jumped out of the van.

"Lauren?" Jamie whispered as he walked around the front of the van toward her. He'd just slipped a baseball cap on. "Would you care to go bowling with me?"

Lauren stared. "Where did you get that?"

Jamie pretended to look innocent. He pointed to the hat. "This? My Yankees cap? I carry it with me everywhere for good luck. And now it's going to fit in nicely with the bowling set. But you . . . well . . ."

Lauren looked down at her oversize denim jacket. A gauzy skirt in a funky pineapple design flared out below, and her red high-top sneakers completed the picture. "I'm wearing the right shoes, aren't I?" she asked innocently.

Jamie reached into the back of the van and pulled out an old baseball jacket. "You're hopeless, Lauren. You *rent* really ugly shoes to bowl in. Okay? Now put this on and do your best to pretend you're my steady girlfriend."

"I'm not ready to wear your ring," Lauren tossed back, trying to relax, even though every muscle in her body was on full alert and her stomach was locked in the spin cycle.

"Fake it, honey," Jamie mocked, grabbing her around the side and steering her toward the front door.

Lauren gave a small laugh. She couldn't help it. It was the only way she could release some of the tension mounting up inside her. Plus, she was starting to like Jamie in a friendly, co-worker kind of way. After all, in the last two days, she'd spent every free moment working on the story with him. She liked his irreverent jokes, his funny stories about journalism school, his quick wit that made her feel accepted—and relaxed.

Lauren stared sadly at the middle line in the highway. Relaxed. Relaxed, the way things used to be between her and Dash, before things got complicated. Before work got in the way. And pride. And jealousy. And the stupid, senseless stubbornness.

"Ladies first, of course." Jamie ushered her into a large, smelly area, covered with stained red carpeting. Lauren cringed. The place smelled like cigarette butts and wet dogs. Plus, it had a huge, 1950s-style domed roof that looked as if it were about to collapse. In the background, she could hear the thunder of bowling balls and the clatter of toppling pins.

"Oh," Jamie murmured, pointing his head to the side. "They're big. They're tough. They bowl."

Lauren's eyes darted across the huge area until she saw Billy and his gang lounging around a circular table, sloshing beer into a bunch of glasses. One of the skinheads had already started to harass a HiTop employee who was wiping off a group of nearby tables.

"Let's try to get the empty lane next to them," Lauren whispered as they stood in line for shoes and bowling balls. "Maybe they'll say something. Anything. I'm getting desperate."

Jamie nodded. "We're white enough for them. Maybe we can all be friends."

Lauren groaned as she took the plastic-looking shoes from Jamie and headed for the alleys. One of the skinheads had just thrown a gutter ball, and his friends were laughing hysterically.

"You throw like a girl, Frankie," Billy cried out, his weird, high-pitched laughter making Lauren's hair stand on end.

"Why, you . . ." Lauren dropped her shoes on the table, clenching her fists and heading for him.

"Lauren." Jamie's voice was in her ear. His hand clutched her elbow and silently pulled her back. "Stop it. You want to get in a fight? Wait until we have our story, okay?"

Lauren's face was hot. "Chauvinist pigs," she muttered under her breath.

"Okay." Jamie stepped into his shoes and began lacing them. Their scorecards and little yellow pencils were placed neatly on the chipped table. "Let's just play and listen," he said in a low voice. He stuck two fingers into the holes of the ball and stood up. "Watch me. You get two balls for each setup."

"Really?" Lauren said, looking toward Billy Jones and his thugs at the next table. She spotted the give-away snake tattoo on the arm of a gang member throwing the ball. Behind him, Billy and the others had quieted. She took an excited breath. They seemed to be hovering over a piece of yellow paper.

"Hey, honey!" Jamie was saying loudly as he came back for another ball. "Did ya see that two-ten split?"

Lauren looked at him and sighed. "Way to go,

sweetheart," she managed with a small wink. "I'm going to look so terrible out there after you."

"No, no," Jamie came back. "Don't talk that way, babykins. You can do it."

Lauren took one of the heavy balls and walked out onto the lane. Just being near Billy Jones made her sick. All she could think of was Dash being thrown into jail because of them.

"Lookin' good," Jamie encouraged. "Don't be afraid, honey. No one's watching."

Lauren rolled her eyes and threw her first ball, which landed with a thud and rolled limply into the gutter. Then as she walked back, feigning disappointment, she looked at Billy again. She narrowed her eyes. He was writing something down now on the yellow paper, as if he were explaining something to his gang members. She absolutely had to see what it was.

". . . little fairies with their . . ." Lauren thought she heard Billy say just before another bowling ball crashed.

". . . be damned if we're gonna stand around while . . . infiltrate our way of . . ."

Lauren couldn't stand it. She was desperate to hear their conversation, but the ear-splitting bowling-alley noises were making it impossible. Slowly, she slid her chair nearer to the group.

". . . do the same thing. It taught them a lesson and now those skinny little fags . . ."

KABOOOM! Jamie leaped into the air, yelling. "A strike! I threw a strike! I don't believe it."

Lauren's eyes were bugging out, annoyed, as she looked at him from the table. She jerked her head sideways toward the gang.

Jamie winced and sat down. "Sorry," he murmured.

For the next half hour, Lauren and Jamie bowled quietly, waiting for the gang to make a move. Finally, all four of the skinheads stood up, gave the place a menacing look, and wandered over to the snack bar.

"Tell me when they look ready to come back," Lauren hissed to Jamie. Her pulse rising, she slowly stood up and walked closer to the gang's deserted table, pretending to watch a nearby game with great intensity. After a few minutes, she nodded with appreciation at the players, then stepped back and pretended to bump against the skinheads' table. Swiftly she grabbed the yellow sheet of paper Billy Jones had been writing on and scanned it desperately.

Frankie, Bob, and Jerry: cocktail duty. Ready by eight o'clock pickup. Glass Slipper windows facing alley. Al parks on 3rd.

The paper had the snake emblem doodled on it, but no last names or phone numbers. A crude map had been drawn, though it was smudged with grease and was difficult to read.

Lauren absorbed the words in horror, but she didn't know what they meant. She shuddered. What was it? Some kind of plan? Another firebombing mission? Were more innocent lives at stake? And with Dash out of jail, would he take the blame again?

"Come on," Jamie warned. "They're going to see you."

Lauren slipped the paper back onto the table. A minute later, she was again pretending to be a cute date, while the skinheads were wolfing down large burgers in their seats.

"You did real well, hon," Jamie said loudly, his eyes darting over to Billy Jones's table, waiting for their next move.

"Thanks, lambykins," Lauren replied, bending her head close to his. "The Glass Slipper," she said in a low voice. "The name sounds familiar, but I can't place it."

"All right!" the skinheads suddenly burst out. Lauren looked over her shoulder as they high-fived one another and raised their fists. Billy Jones let out one of his crazy laughs. Then he grabbed the hand of another gang member and began a spontaneous arm wrestle over a basket of french fries, which spilled on the floor. ". . . little spic . . . fell right into our hands . . . can take the rap for the sweet little job we did on the fancy sorority liberals and their Nee-gro poet."

Quickly, Lauren turned away. She couldn't breathe.

Dash.

They were gloating over Dash taking the rap for the firebombing.

Lauren gripped Jamie's arm, trying to control herself. She wanted to fling insults on these creeps. She wanted to kick and shout and hurt them. Her body felt like a furnace of pure rage.

"What is it?" Jamie whispered. "What did you hear?"

Lauren shook her head in quick little movements, willing the hot tears to stay back. She was actually sitting ten feet away from the people who were destroying Dash's life. It was almost too much to bear.

The Glass Slipper.

That name kept running through her mind. What was it?

"Hey." Jamie was tapping her arm. "They're leaving. Get your stuff."

Lauren watched the skinhead gang amble into the lobby and yank the door open. Then she and Jamie stood up and raced to dump their rented equipment on the counter. Taking deep breaths, they opened the front door and strolled into the bowling alley's parking lot.

Across the pavement, Lauren could see Billy Jones sprawled on the hood of his station wagon, shooting the breeze with the other three, his face screwed into a crazy, stupid grin.

Lauren was determined to stick with them, even if she risked making them suspicious. She walked forward, clinging to Jamie's arm as if they were leaving a fun date. There had to be something else she could take away from this awful place. A word. A clue.

"My wallet!" Lauren suddenly said in a voice loud enough for the entire parking lot to hear. By that time, she and Jamie were only a few feet away from the station wagon. They were close. Very close.

She stopped abruptly, and began digging through her purse. "Let me see . . ." Lauren pretended.

The skinheads looked her way for a moment, then turned back. Their voices rose into the dark night.

". . . fags are spreading a goddamned foreign plague through our country, and we're going to let them know we don't appreciate it," Billy was ranting.

Lauren froze. It sounded like Billy's latest problem was with homosexuals. Was there any end to his madness? "It must be here somewhere . . ." she muttered, still digging through her purse.

Jamie pretended to be concerned. "Maybe you left it inside."

". . . left-wing liberal college agitators want to give them money. I say we beat the crap out of all of them. Maybe surprise them with a few cocktails, too." Billy sneered.

Lauren's knees buckled. "Oh, my God," she whispered, finally realizing what Billy was talking about.

Billy and his gang were planning to disrupt tomorrow night's AIDS benefit. The Glass Slipper. Now she remembered. The downtown disco where it would take place.

They're going to beat people up and throw the same Molotov cocktails they used on the Tri Beta house! Lauren thought, horrified.

"Don't get all upset, pumpkin," Jamie said, still trying to keep up their act. His arms were circling Lauren as if he wanted to shield her from whatever deadly plan Billy Jones was hatching. "Do you know what it all means?" he whispered.

Lauren nodded. "I found it, honey!" she managed to call out, waving her wallet in the air as Jamie dragged her away. "It was there all along and I just didn't see it!"

Eleven

Faith was trying to steady herself.

"Is that grocery bag too heavy for you?" Merideth was asking over his shoulder. "I can get someone from the Colin's House staff to come out and help."

"Oh—um—no," Faith stammered, quickening her pace up the walkway that led to a well kept ranch house surrounded by trimmed shrubs and a wide green lawn.

Merideth waited for her patiently near the door, though he could barely see over the three huge grocery bags he was hauling into the Colin's House kitchen. Faith knew Merideth didn't want to rush her. She knew he didn't want her to be afraid. Even his happy-go-lucky, polka-dot suspenders seemed to say, *Relax, Faith. Everything's okay.*

"Got it?" Merideth winked at her.

Faith gulped, nodded, then gave a determined smile. Her cowboy boots clicked past a row of potted geraniums and on up the porch steps. On the outside, she was the same patient, only-too-happy-to-help Faith. On the inside, her heart was caving in, her bones were shaking, and her mouth was dry. Suddenly, inexplicably, she was terrified of being an AIDS volunteer.

"You okay?" Merideth said in a low voice as she neared. Ahead, Robert was opening the front door.

"Why do you ask?" Faith said almost too quickly.

"I don't know," Merideth apologized. "It's just that it's your first visit here. Sometimes it's tough."

"No problem," Faith lied, jamming the heavy bag up with her hip to readjust the weight. She took a breath and pushed the terror down somewhere into the pit of her stomach.

"Come on in, dear," a woman's friendly voice was saying.

Faith hesitated in the front entry. Up ahead in the main room, a group of sofas was arranged around a television set and a coffee table piled with books and magazines. There was a hall to her left and a homey-looking kitchen on her right, where a large woman was busily helping Merideth and Robert unload the groceries.

Faith gulped.

"Thank you so much," the woman was saying, taking the grocery bags.

"Sarah?" Merideth said. "This is Faith Crowley—a friend from U of S. She's interested in volunteering."

"Wonderful," Sarah replied, busily pulling cans out of the bag and setting them in a high cupboard. Her lacquered hairstyle was shaped neatly about her fifty-something face, and her lips wore a bright shade of red lipstick.

Faith looked nervously over her shoulder. A frail man moved slowly down the hall, supported by a walker with rubber-tipped legs. She looked away shyly and stuffed her hands in her jeans pockets, trying to think of something to say.

A bell rang in the distance, and Sarah headed down the hall. Faith leaned against the kitchen counter and watched helplessly as Robert and Merideth unloaded groceries. Faith's eyes darted over the squeaky-clean kitchen. A large number of prescription bottles were stacked on the open shelves near the refrigerator, and a box of disposable plastic gloves sat near the sink. Near the door to the hall was a stainless-steel serving cart with a bowl of partly eaten applesauce on it.

Faith was starting to feel dizzy. A rubbery, menthol smell filled the air. She paled. It was a sickroom smell. Urine. Disinfectants. Death.

"Faith?" Merideth walked over and touched her shoulder.

"No." Faith steadied herself. "No. I'm okay."

"Well, another new volunteer today," Sarah said, moving briskly back into the kitchen. She picked up the applesauce dish and rinsed it in the sink. Faith turned toward her and made herself breathe. She wasn't going to fall apart. She had come here to help, and she was here to stay.

"Yes," Faith blurted. "Please. Tell me what I can do."

Sarah smiled, turning and looking Faith in the eyes. "The best thing you can do is talk to some of our residents, Faith. They may be too weak to chat much, but it's company."

"Fine," Faith said, a nervous buzz building up in her throat like her first day in the debate club at Lewis and Clark High. She coughed, trying to still the quavery sound. A pot of something that smelled strange was boiling on the stove, and Sarah turned down the gas flame.

"I hear you came up with the danceathon idea for the fund-raiser," Sarah spoke up, grabbing a pot holder. "It's great. We'd like to hire another full-time nurse with the proceeds."

"I hope you can," Faith replied in a tiny voice, wondering if she should just wander around the hospice now and look for someone to talk to. But what would she say? What could she possibly say?

"Sarah's got things under control," Merideth said, shutting a cupboard door. "Sign in here, then we'll go meet a friend of mine."

Faith nodded as he directed her toward the

Colin's House guest book at the end of the kitchen counter. Taking the pen, she carefully signed in, noting the time she arrived. Then she saw something that made her start. Just above her name was written: *Courtney Conner. 8 a.m.-10:30 a.m.*

"Courtney?" Faith murmured out loud. Courtney Conner, princess of sorority row?

"What, dear?" Sarah said over her shoulder.

"Courtney Conner," Faith stumbled, picking up the sign-in pencil. "I—I know her. Sort of. But I didn't know she was a volunteer here."

"Came in for the first time today," Sarah explained. "She was a lovely girl and very helpful. In fact, she read the morning paper to several people."

Faith clenched her teeth, more determined than ever to muster every scrap of courage she had. If Courtney could come in here and help people with this terrible disease, she could too.

"Come on," Merideth said in a low voice. "There's someone I'd like you to meet. His name is Casey."

"Okay," Faith said timidly, signing her name quickly and closing the book.

Merideth rubbed the side of his face and spoke quietly. "He's a good guy. Family doesn't visit. Not many friends. Apparently got the HIV virus when he was an IV-drug user."

"Mmmmm." Faith nodded. She looked down at her hands. A Band-Aid on her palm covered the tiny puncture wound she had gotten thumbtacking danceathon posters all over campus. She looked at it, then looked at it again, panicked. Before this instant, she hadn't thought about the need for protection. She looked over at the disposable gloves. Would they ask her to change a urine bag, or a dressing, or a . . . ?

"You'll like him," Merideth was saying, guiding her out to the living room.

Faith steadied herself. She had to get through this. After all, she could always wear the gloves if she thought she was in the slightest danger. Plus, the HIV virus wasn't something you could get from casual contact, like talking to someone, or shaking someone's hand. Faith slowed her breathing and unclenched her hands.

This is ridiculous, Faith thought. *People with AIDS are* people. *They don't want to be here. They don't want to be sick. And they don't deserve to die.*

Merideth and Faith moved ahead into the living room, where Robert was already talking to a thin young man in a wheelchair who was watching television. Music played in the background, and bunches of homemade flower arrangements dotted the tables.

Across the room, a pale young man sat quietly near the window in a wheelchair.

"Casey?" Merideth said in a low voice, placing his hand on the guy's thin shoulder.

Slowly, and with great effort, Casey set his hands down on the wheels of his chair and turned it around. Faith's knees began to buckle, so she slipped a casual hand on Merideth's arm to keep from falling. Casey was a graying wisp of a man. His face was a mask that had shrunk down onto his fragile skull, and his translucent skin was covered with brown and red oval spots. Under his pajamas, Faith could see that his legs had emaciated into two brittle sticks. It took all of her self-control to keep from running out of the room.

"Hello," Casey said weakly, his pale eyes drifting up. "Good to see you, Merideth."

Merideth stepped aside a little. "Hey, Casey. This is my friend, Faith Crowley from U of S. She's into the theater like me—and she came up with the danceathon idea for tomorrow night's fund-raiser."

"Hi, Casey," Faith said gently, watching Casey extend his shaky hand, so thin and bony she could practically see the light filtering through it. As she shook it, she saw that it was veined and spotted like her grandmother's. "Very nice to meet you."

A burly man in a white uniform stepped into the room with a tray of pills and a glass of water. Merideth reached over and flipped up a small table attached to Casey's wheelchair.

"Thanks," Casey said shakily. Faith stared at the pills rolling around on the tray, listening to her chest pound.

"Uh, Faith," Merideth spoke up. "There's someone else I'm going to say hello to. Catch you in a minute."

"Okay," Faith muttered, her eyes clinging to Merideth as he walked out of the room. Then slowly she turned toward Casey and sat down in the chair next to him. Two hours. She had signed up for two hours. How would she get through it?

"Your first time here?" Casey began softly, panting a little, as if he was having a hard time breathing. He picked a pill off the tray and lifted the water cup shakily to his lips.

"Is that better?" the male nurse was saying loudly behind them. Faith turned around. The nurse had plugged in a small fan in front of another man in a wheelchair.

"Steven gets hot," Casey said in a tired monotone. "He's also blind."

"Oh, I see," Faith managed.

"I get cold," he explained, lifting his limp hand slightly to point at the shawl around his shoulders. "Not sure why. Maybe the medication."

"Yeah, maybe the medication," Faith repeated stupidly. She looked away. His thin face was horrible. It reminded her of KC's dad dying of lung cancer. It reminded her of her grandmother dying of pneumonia. Casey had that same disconnected look in his eyes, as if his spirit had already left this world and his body was just waiting patiently to join him. Mr. Angeletti had had that look just before he died. And her grandmother, too. Only, Casey had to be in his twenties; that was what made it so unreal.

Casey gave her a weak smile, lifting one gray eyebrow a little. "You're in the theater?"

Faith nodded. She tried to think. "Yes. My big love. I like it in big doses, little doses. I even sit through the bad stuff and enjoy it."

Casey's dry lips parted a little, as if he were catching his breath, or perhaps laughing softly. "The bad stuff?"

"Well, I mean . . ." Faith started to explain.

"That's—how—you learn."

"Uh-huh." Faith narrowed her eyebrows and nodded, trying to follow.

"I guess that's how you figure out how a play works." Casey struggled to get the words out. "See the bad stuff too."

Faith smiled, and a rush of relief raced through her head. "Yes. Yes, you're absolutely right."

Casey's sad eyes seemed to sink back inside of him. "A danceathon. Good idea."

"Thank you. I think it'll be a lot of fun. And—well, I don't know why I'm having such a hard time saying this . . . but people really do . . . care, you know."

A small, disbelieving smile appeared on Casey's face. "Thanks for saying that."

"Well, it's true," Faith came back, almost hotly, searching for a focus. Courage. Strength. Anything to propel her through this conversation.

"I was in a dance contest once," Casey said suddenly.

"Really?"

"I did a rap number," Casey said, wheezing. He stopped to catch his breath and struggled to grab the end of his shoulder blanket, which was slipping off.

Quickly Faith reached over and draped it into place.

"Thanks," Casey whispered, panting again. "You should have seen us. Waggling elbows, kicking feet, all that. God, we were great." He sighed and looked out the window.

"A good memory?" Faith asked gently.

"Oh, yeah," Casey said dreamily. "I felt so— alive."

Faith paused, waiting for him to finish. She watched as he closed his eyes dreamily, and for a minute she thought he'd fallen asleep.

"It's—such a—good—vi—bra—tion," Casey made a feeble, hoarse attempt to sing. *"It's such a sweeeeet sensation . . ."*

Faith nodded in wonder. "I know it. Maybe we'll play that tomorrow night in your honor."

"I'd like that, Faith."

"Then it's done."

There was another long silence as Faith sat there, twisting the end of her braid, looking out the window. Casey seemed so sweet and sad, as if he'd lost all of his anger and fear. It seemed wrong to be afraid next to someone with so much courage.

Especially when he was the one who was dying— not her.

Faith bit her lip. She was having a hard time adjusting. Death wasn't something she thought about very much. Maybe she should. Maybe if she thought more about how her life had a beginning and an end, she'd think more about what she was doing with her time. It was too late for Casey, but it wasn't for her.

"May I . . . help you with anything today?" Faith offered, rubbing the tops of her soft jeans.

"Sure," Casey replied slowly. His bony hands struggled with the wheels of his chair. "I—uh . . ."

Faith instinctively reached out. "Please. Let me."

"I have a few letters," Casey began. His face looked confused and weary. "I think Sarah's keeping them for me, and I . . ."

"I'll get them for you," Faith replied briskly, standing up. A few seconds later she returned with three envelopes and a postcard. "Okay," she began. "Here's one with a return address that says Vivian Shaw, Sisters, Oregon."

"Vivian," Casey whispered, languidly fingering the ends of his bathrobe tie. His head fell over weakly to the side. "I met Vivian in the University of Springfield library right after I tested positive for the HIV virus."

"The library?" Faith asked gently.

Casey let out a long sigh, his thin fingers fiddling with the edge of his robe. "The library. I was in a panic, of course—after I got the news. So I . . . spent all of my time in the library—reading about the disease. The treatments. The people who survived for years—with healthy habits."

"And Vivian?" Faith asked quietly as Casey fell silent, apparently forgetting his train of thought.

"Yeah," Casey said tiredly. "She was an herbalist and masseuse. We became friends."

"Yes."

"She . . . helped me turn my life around," Casey went on, stronger, lifting his chin and smiling into the distance. "I became a vegetarian and learned how to relax. Got a job as a technical writer for one of those hip, rich software manufacturers. Things were going great. I felt great. So many people think you're sick when you get HIV, but you can go for a long time without any AIDS symptoms."

There was a long silence as Casey fell out of the conversation into his own world. Faith timidly slipped her finger under the envelope flap and took out Vivian's letter. "Do you want me to read it, Casey?" she whispered. "I—"

"Okay now, stop here," came Merideth's voice.

Faith turned around and watched him help a sparrowlike woman down the step into the living room. Gripped in his other hand was a metal stand that held a dangling intravenous bag that was attached to an IV in her arm.

"W-w-wait!" Merideth cried softly. "You're getting ahead of me."

"Don't slow me down, Mr. Do-gooder," the woman joked, obviously enjoying the attention. Her blond hair was stringy, and she wore a faded bathrobe around her stick-thin body, but her eyes were full of humor and intelligence. "I feel good today."

"You're not just feeling good. You're a crazy woman," Merideth joked.

"I'm not crazy, Merideth," the woman shot back, heading for the nearest chair. "My ex-boyfriend was. He's the one who slept with every woman in town—then had the nerve to keep coming back to me. He said he didn't know he had the virus. But if I'd known what he was doing out there, I could have told him myself: The chances are pretty good you do, you fool."

Faith looked down at her boots and drew in her breath sharply. That woman could have been her. Or Winnie. Or any woman who'd had unprotected sex. Her eyes began to feel hot and watery, and she struggled to keep from breaking down. The thought terrified her.

"Would you help me back to my room, Faith?" Casey was asking her. He'd closed his eyes and his hands had fallen back into his lap.

"Oh, sure," Faith replied, gathering the letters. She stood up, reached for the handles on his wheelchair, and pushed him toward the hall. "Tell me when to turn," she reminded him.

Faith's eyes darted warily into several of the rooms. She saw one nurse turning a very thin young man in his bed, his arms hanging limply at his sides. In another room, a guy lay perfectly still, staring at the ceiling, a plastic tube extending out of his chest.

"Thanks," Casey panted as Faith helped him onto his bed. He rested his head back on the flowered pillowcase. "You doing okay so far? This place gets to some people."

"Sure," Faith said shakily. "I guess I'm better than I was when I first walked in. But it's hard . . ."

Casey shrugged a little, then slowly lifted his pale eyes toward her. "My parents don't come. They know where I am, but I guess they can't accept what's happened."

"I'm sorry."

"Yeah," Casey responded slowly. "Well, they were happy when I straightened my life out and got the job with the software company. But when I started to get sick a few months later and told them about getting AIDS, they lost it."

Faith shook her head, resting her hip against the side of his bed.

"It's a strange disease," Casey struggled. "First you lose your job because you're too sick to work. So you lose your apartment. Then you have to tell people why—and they bolt because they're scared. You end up losing everything. If it hadn't been for Colin's House, I'd have nowhere to go."

Faith watched sadly as Casey's eyes started to close. "Sleep well," she whispered, reaching out to fold his sheet back smoothly over his chest. She straightened his blanket and gathered his soft shawl closer around his neck. She stood up to go, then stopped, unable to hold back. Casey's life. One minute it was here. The next minute it could be gone. Tears slipped down her face.

For the next two hours, Faith worked nonstop. She read the sports page to the guy who'd lost his sight to AIDS. She fed Jell-O to another guy whose mouth was riddled with ulcers. She helped with medical-insurance forms. She held hands.

By the time her shift was over, her muscles ached, her head was pounding, and she was ready to go home. It was about six o'clock, and as she walked down the hall, Faith could see Sarah pouring her homemade soup into bowls arranged on a series of bed trays.

Faith slowed when she saw Merideth near the kitchen door, his ear bent into a telephone receiver, his fingers anxiously twisting the cord.

"Okay, yeah," he murmured softly into the phone as he put it down.

Faith stopped, curious.

Robert was standing close to him, his arms crossed in front of his chest, as if he were absorbing bad news. Faith frowned to herself and remained frozen against the wall in the hallway. What had happened? She looked over again, her heart climbing into her throat. Merideth and Robert were both staring sadly at the floor.

". . . health center," Merideth said too softly for

Faith to completely hear. ". . . HIV test result . . ."

Faith clamped her back hard against the wall.

". . . positive . . ."

Her hand flew up to her mouth.

". . . can't believe it . . ."

Faith's heart was dropping like a stone now. When she looked over again, she could see that Robert had stepped forward and wrapped his arms around Merideth, who had turned white.

Merideth?

Merideth with the HIV virus?

Faith thought back desperately. Then she remembered that Merideth had been expecting his HIV-virus test result any day now. She couldn't breathe. Merideth? *Her* Merideth? Was he going to have to suffer like Casey and the rest?

Faith spotted a bathroom across the hallway and ducked inside. She shut the door behind her, locked it, and sat down on the toilet-seat lid, sobbing into her hands.

Doesn't anyone see? The world is going crazy, she thought bitterly. *People are dying. People who are too young to die.*

Faith couldn't get up. She couldn't do anything but sit in the cold bathroom, feeling her heart break and letting go of the tears she'd been holding back for too long.

Twelve

osh was running a finger under his tight collar. "Then you *are* fairly familiar with the Word 5.0 system and the IBM PC hardware?" a prim woman wearing a white shirt and bow tie was asking him. Her salt-and-pepper hair hung in a sharp line along her jaw.

Josh shifted in his seat, taking in her monochrome office decor. Black desk. Gray file cabinet. One abstract print. One large potted ficus plant in the corner.

After his recent confrontation with the Gaffey-Gottlieb budget, Josh had made a trip down to the U of S Job Center and answered an ad for a weekend word-processing position at a local law firm.

"Yeah," Josh replied, trying to sound enthusiastic. The place was a little eerie, with its harsh overhead lights and black and gray noncolor schemes. "I know the old Shift-Control-Alt. The 'F' keys. Cryptic, in a way, isn't it? I suppose it stands for function. A fairly bad word-processing software system, in terms of training requirements, but you can have a lot of fun with it once you get the—uh—hang of it."

Josh paused, then looked down. The woman was looking with dismay at Josh's hairy white ankle bopping up and down on his knee. She touched one of her gold earrings nervously.

"In fact," Josh said, trying to ignore her, "a bunch of us made up a little Word Trivial Pursuit game that we play for laughs once in a while at the computer center. The trick is to memorize as many functions as possible."

The woman was giving him a strange look.

Okay, so I forgot my socks, Josh thought, frustrated. *Who cares? They want to me to type into a computer, not dress like my dad.*

"Mr. Gaffey," she began crisply, lacing her fingers in front of her, her elbows planted firmly on the desk. A plastic container near her hands was bristling with razor-sharp pencils. "I have been personnel manager for the firm of Hoskins, Stempler, and Bremen for exactly five years now."

"Gee, that's—"

"And I have never," she interrupted, "seen a

word-processing score as high as yours."

Josh lifted his hands up and wiggled his fingers. "They leap tall buildings in a single bound. Run faster than a locomotive . . ."

"That is why we would be willing to offer you a part-time weekend position at a salary of nine dollars per hour," the woman continued. "We would require your services between noon and nine P.M. Saturday and Sunday, with an hour lunch. You would prepare correspondence and legal briefs from dictation provided to you on audio tapes."

Josh quickly calculated. *Sixteen hours per week, times nine dollars, is a hundred and forty-four. Times four weekends, that would be more than five hundred and seventy-five dollars per month.*

"I wish to remind you that there are several other qualified candidates, but we feel that your expertise with this particular word-processing system will be more helpful if we experience system breakdowns."

"I can fix anything!" Josh exclaimed.

"Fine, then." The woman rose, revealing a gray pleated skirt. Her blue eyes slid carefully over Josh's wrinkled button-down, dark cords, and loafers, then moved to the file cabinet. She drew out a folder containing a large number of documents. "I'll need you to fill these out by tomorrow, when you start." She turned around and gave him a stern look. "You can start tomorrow, then?"

"Yeah, fine," Josh said happily. Sure, it would be tough to spend that much time away from Winnie on the weekends. But at least he'd found a relatively painless way to collect a little badly needed money.

"Come this way, please," the woman instructed, opening the door for him. Josh automatically slapped his Oakland A's baseball hat on backward and began ambling down the sterile hallway, trying not to breathe the inky office smells too deeply. He peered curiously into the boxy offices as they passed. Each one seemed oddly bare. One woman sat perfectly still as she read something on her desk. In another office, a guy was scratching his head and rolling his eyes as he talked into the telephone.

"Partners' offices are down that way." The woman pointed past a huge front desk, armed with a large switchboard and a dangerous-looking receptionist wearing a red dress. "And word processing is over here."

Josh stuffed his hands in his pockets and glanced to the side. Expensively framed art was everywhere, and the furniture looked as if it had been upholstered in pinstriped suits. Through the wall of a glassed-in meeting room, he could see a group of men in suits shaking their heads, talking about something.

Five hundred and seventy-six dollars a month! A fortune! Josh told himself. *If we save that amount for the next six months, we'll have almost thirty-five hundred dollars to cover extra expenses.*

"And here we are." The woman stopped in front of a gray door and swept her hand in cheerily.

Josh looked inside and felt his face drop.

The room was a windowless cell, about six by ten feet, containing nothing but a desk, a chair, a word processor, and a few manuals on the shelf above. "Gee," Josh started to joke, a cold sweat breaking out on his back. "What a glorious view."

"Most of our word processors prefer to work alone with as little distraction as possible," the woman said, stepping back.

"Well," Josh muttered sarcastically. "That's one thing they won't get in here. No distraction whatsoever."

"And another thing, Mr. Gaffey."

"Yes?" Josh looked at her small face and carefully styled hair.

"A suit and tie are required apparel at Hoskins, Stempler, and Bremen."

Josh stared at her as he felt his life slip out of his reach. "On weekends?"

"A professional look must be maintained even on weekends." The personnel director gave him a businesslike smile. "You are an employee of the firm. People see you entering and leaving the building. It's our corporate image we're talking about. And it's quite important to the partnership."

"Oh."

"One more thing."

"Yes?" Josh felt like he needed air. Supporting a baby was one thing. But giving up his life, his freedom, his dignity—that was another. Was he making a huge mistake?

"The earring."

Josh stiffened. He self-consciously reached up to the tiny blue stone he wore in one ear. "The earring," he repeated, giving it a twirl.

"Yes. Please leave the earring at home."

There was an anxious rustling of skirts on the Tri Beta patio as KC and her sisters waited for Courtney to appear. It was ten o'clock Saturday morning, and the spring sunshine was filtering pleasantly through the stately maples. The smell of fresh paint wafted out of the house. A workman was hammering away in the living room.

KC sat nervously at the edge of the group, fingering her leather day organizer.

Since leaving Courtney in front of the post office earlier that week, she hadn't seen Courtney for even a moment.

Courtney had missed the Friday morning wallpaper-picking breakfast.

She'd skipped last night's barbecue event hosted by the sympathetic Gammas.

And so far, she'd failed to let anyone know about Mrs. Wiley's three-thousand-dollar contribution.

"Hi, everyone!" Courtney said breezily, finally bursting through the French doors onto the terrace. KC stared at her. Not only was her hair still tied back in a grubby bandanna, but she wore a pair of railroad-engineer overalls that obscured her slim figure and made her look like a sack of potatoes.

There was stony silence as Courtney plopped down on a chair and rapidly read through something in her notebook. Someone cleared her throat.

"Thanks for coming, everyone," Courtney said, absently tugging the knot on her bandanna.

"What's up, Courtney?" Diane asked. "Couldn't we have handled this last night at the Gamma barbecue?"

Courtney's chin rose, and her eyes were chilly as they met Diane's. "I was going to come, Diane. But there was an emergency at the Springfield Community Center, and I couldn't attend."

Diane's face was stone. "I see."

KC watched as Courtney looked away, her face artificially brightening. "We've had a generous and unexpected donation," she announced, cheerfully waving Mrs. Wiley's pink envelope.

A murmur of approval rippled through the group, and KC let out a breath of relief.

"Mrs. Wiley has given the Tri Beta house an unconditional donation of three thousand dollars," Courtney continued. "But, as you know, our insurance has covered nearly all renovation expenses."

"Then why am I spending all of my free time ruining my nails?" one of the girls hissed loudly.

Courtney held up her hand for quiet as a dozen shiny heads began murmuring in agreement. "Your nails are ruined, Debbie," Courtney said in a withering tone, "because the insurance does not cover cleanup and finishing costs, such as wallpaper and painting. I've already told you this."

"Thanks for explaining again," Debbie snarled back.

"Therefore," Courtney said, businesslike, "I have an idea I'd like to share with you."

KC stiffened. Whatever Courtney's idea was, she had the feeling it still wasn't going to be a gazebo, or a swimming pool, or a new rose garden.

"As you all know," Courtney began eagerly, "a group of concerned students on campus is organizing a danceathon tonight at The Glass Slipper to raise money for Springfield's only AIDS hospice—Colin's House."

A few girls squirmed. The rest stared. Marcia Tabbert's glossy mouth had dropped open in horror.

Winnie, KC thought. *Winnie got to her. Courtney wants to take that money and give it away to dying AIDS patients. The girls will never understand.*

"Yesterday morning," Courtney continued, her brown eyes burning with conviction, "I had the privilege of volunteering for a couple of hours at the hospice."

"Courtney," Marcia exclaimed, "are you sure that's safe? I mean, aren't you bringing back all sorts of germs and—"

"Don't be ridiculous," Courtney said sharply. "AIDS is a sexually transmitted disease."

"She's right," Diane said irritably, propping her chin up with two hands and staring up at the sky.

"It's a terribly important cause," Courtney continued. "Colin's House is for AIDS patients who have nowhere else to turn when they're sick. I could hand them this check tonight at the danceathon. What do you say?"

KC's mouth dropped open. She had been there when Courtney pulled the check out of the envelope. Mrs. Wiley wanted her money to be used for the Tri Beta house. Courtney was her friend and her most powerful connection on campus, but she had to say something.

"Excuse me, Courtney," KC said sharply, springing to her feet.

Courtney turned, and for a moment, the two friends were locked in a confusing exchange of looks.

"That money," KC finally said, her voice shaking, "was specifically intended for the Tri Beta house. I was there when you read Mrs. Wiley's letter."

"*What?*" several sisters who hadn't heard about the donation cried out.

Courtney set her jaw and stared straight at KC, her eyes blazing. "Our expenses have been covered, KC—and Colin's House desperately needs funds."

"Send the money back, then," KC said. "We have no right to use Mrs. Wiley's money any way we please."

"KC," Courtney pleaded.

"This is outrageous!" Diane called out, standing up and casting her eyes angrily about the group, as if she were looking for support.

"In fact," KC said, staring at Courtney, "Mrs.

Wiley specifically suggested we use the money to build a gazebo for the garden. It was her explicit intention to do something nice for us."

"And we should be thanking her for being so generous," one of the freshman pledges said out loud.

"Instead of throwing it away on those people with AIDS," another sister called bitterly. "Everyone knows insurance covers people like that."

"As a matter of fact, insurance does not cover *people like that*," Courtney shot back. Her eyes were wide and her cheeks pink with frustration. "I *know* Mrs. Wiley would support us," Courtney added.

KC felt hot tears in the back of her eyes. "That's up to Mrs. Wiley. Not you! You—you haven't been up-front."

"That's right!" several sisters shouted.

"It's her money—and ours—and you're using it for your own purposes," KC went on.

"KC!" Courtney's voice rose and cracked. Her mouth fell open as if she were going to say something, but nothing came out.

The Tri Beta girls drew in a collective breath, their heads bobbing back and forth between KC and Courtney. The terrace was suddenly a beehive of astonished whispering.

"Wait a minute," Courtney cried out, springing up and planting her hands on her hips. "None of you have even been to Colin's House. They desperately need our help!"

"Then some of us will go to the danceathon

tonight, Courtney," KC said. "And it will be our own free choice."

"KC's right," someone shouted as Courtney narrowed her eyes in fury.

"Let's put our own lives back in order before we reach out to the community," KC argued. "Our home has been destroyed and it needs repairing. Maybe you and a few others are cozy and comfortable over at Mrs. Gomez's mansion. But Annie and many others are sleeping on dormitory floors all over this campus."

"She's right!" Diane declared.

KC looked over and saw Courtney's eyes move sharply in her direction, then ice over. Her heart sank. Right then, she knew her friendship with Courtney would never be the same.

"Wait a minute," said Regina Charles, a straight-A prelaw student from a wealthy Texas family. "I think Courtney has a point. If the donation from Mrs. Wiley didn't have any strings attached, Courtney should be allowed to suggest a charity."

Some of the girls nodded in agreement, while a large contingent of the younger pledges were furiously shaking their heads and complaining. KC watched in horror as the meeting took on the quality of a vicious boxing match, with Courtney in one corner and herself in the other.

"I agree," Cameron Dokey, another upperclass sister, called out over the noise. "It's a worthy cause. Courtney's just making a suggestion."

"She's trying to railroad us into it," Diane declared, standing up with a menacing glare. "KC just said that Mrs. Wiley strongly urged us to use the money for a gazebo."

"I'm not railroading anyone," Courtney blazed back. "Open your eyes to those in need. That's all I'm asking."

"Okay, if you insist," Diane interrupted. "I propose putting Courtney's idea to a vote. All those in favor of giving Mrs. Wiley's three-thousand-dollar donation to Colin's House, please raise your hands."

There was a brief, strained silence as a few of the older girls, including Regina and Cameron, raised their hands into the air.

"All opposed?" Diane said defiantly, shooting her own hand up.

At least two-thirds of the group did the same.

So did KC, though the last thing she wanted to do was start a war. But war it was. There were principles involved, and she couldn't back down. Courtney had been overzealous about the money. She'd been wrong. KC moved her eyes miserably toward Courtney and saw that her friend's face had stiffened in anger and shock.

Courtney had made a rare miscalculation. And she had been surprised by it.

"Okay," Diane said with authority, putting a hand on KC's shoulder. "I wish to put another proposal to a vote. I hereby nominate KC Angeletti to replace Courtney Conner as head of the rebuilding committee."

KC froze.

Courtney's mouth dropped open. She stood up and backed away a little.

"That's right," Diane shouted.

"What?" KC started to protest, trying to move out from under Diane's grip. Diane was getting out of hand. Everything was spinning out of control.

"All those in favor?" Diane persisted.

A large group of slim arms rose, and KC stood up—stunned.

"Against?"

Only a few hands rose meekly into the air.

"There you have it, then," Diane declared. "KC's a sharp, organized Tri Beta sister who will serve us well. And now Courtney will have more free time to devote to her many charitable causes."

Courtney angrily gathered her things and began to march toward the door.

KC broke away. She and Courtney had to talk. She didn't want to make an enemy of her friend.

"I'd like to make another proposal," Marcia suddenly cried out over the noise.

KC stopped and gave Marcia a desperate look over her shoulder.

"I propose that KC attend the Colin's House danceathon tonight," Marcia barked. "Just to make sure Courtney doesn't hand over Mrs. Wiley's cash to the AIDS people."

"Done," Diane said just as Courtney slammed the door behind her.

"Courtney!" KC cried out, flinging open the French door and rushing into the empty room. She heard footsteps running over the drop cloths, then the crash of the front door slamming.

KC stopped, paralyzed with dread. Courtney would never forgive her. She'd never understand. All KC could do was stand there alone in the dusty, half-finished hallway, feeling the tears begin to tumble down her face. It was all over. Their friendship was destroyed.

After a few horrible moments, KC felt a hand slipping onto her shoulder and a familiar, light voice next to her.

"I know," Annie murmured. "Someone had to stop her. It's too bad it had to be you."

"She'll never forgive me," KC wailed, turning her wet face to Annie's.

"Give it some time, KC," Annie comforted her, hooking her arm into KC's and leading her toward the front door. Her long floral skirt swished through the silence, and her dangle earrings tinkled. She pulled a tissue out of her straw bag and handed it to her. "Let's go."

KC blew her nose and numbly followed Annie out through the front door. "I can't believe this. Is it the fire?" KC asked in wonder. "Is it Courtney? Is it me?"

Annie patted KC on the back as they headed

down the sidewalk past two workmen carrying a stack of lumber into the house. "Maybe it's a little of everything. This isn't a good time for any of us."

"Tell me about it." KC sighed. "I think I'll stop by the station and see if Cody is there."

"A pair of waiting arms." Annie smiled.

"Yeah," KC said, her eyes filling with tears. "I'm ready to fall right into them and stay there for the rest of the day."

"Good. I've got an errand downtown. But I'll be back at the room in an hour or so."

"Where are you going?"

"Oh, just to the Red Cross. Then I want to stop by the art department," Annie said. "I'm supposed to be hearing about an internship I applied for to study in Rome. I'll bring some coffee back with me."

"Great. But if I don't get back to the room today, let's plan to meet there at nine fifteen," KC said. "We'll go to the danceathon together."

"Good," Annie agreed. "No worries. No regrets. No heavy hearts. Tonight, let's just forget everything else but the music and the stars and the moon and the good-looking guys."

Thirteen

*S*creeeeeeeeeeeeeeech.

Faith jumped, holding her heart, as someone adjusted The Glass Slipper's sound system. She finished pinning a silver streamer to the ceiling, then climbed back down the ladder to the dance floor.

Collapsing on the bottom rung, Faith looked down numbly at her grubby work jeans. She hadn't slept the night before. And for the last eight hours, she'd been scrubbing and decorating the club like a madwoman.

Nuhhhh, the power system buzzed.

What was she supposed to do next? Faith couldn't remember. All around her, there was laughter, excitement—music. But since she'd overheard the news about Merideth's HIV-virus test yesterday afternoon, nothing was making any sense to her.

Merideth sick? Merideth with AIDS? Merideth—gone?

Faith pressed her dry, cracked lips together. She couldn't break down now. She had to wait. Everyone expected her to take charge of this event and make it a success. And that's exactly what she was going to do. It was the only thing she *could* do. She didn't care that her hands were punctured from the countless tacks. Or that her face was covered with poster paint and floor wax. Her mind was focused like a steel vise on the success of this night.

It was the one thing she could control right now.

"We've got rap, seventies disco, sixties freestyle," Kimberly Dayton said, rattling off the list of danceathon categories.

"Don't forget jitterbug, tango, swing, and the swim," Liza Ruff blared down from her ladder as she stapled another Mylar streamer to the ceiling. Her skintight orange jumpsuit revealed every inch of her ample hips, and her red hair flared out of a glittery headband.

"Come on," complained track champion Melissa McDormand, who was busily setting up chairs around the elegant tables, her ankle wrapped in an Ace bandage. "No one knows how to do those steps."

"Are you for real?" Kimberly joked, throwing her long dancer's body into a backward tango drop. "Half the U of S dance department has been rehearsing for five days straight. They're *dying* to show off."

Faith checked her watch. Countdown: two hours until the doors opened. She looked around, her head feeling disconnected from her body. At least the place looked wonderful. And money from brisk advance-ticket sales was pouring in. Then she let her eyes slip across the room to Merideth, who was attempting to sing an Irish ballad while wiping glassware behind the bar. Right beside him was Robert, arranging bar stools and shining up the counter. She was going to have to talk to Merideth soon.

She had to tell him what she knew.

"I keep thinking of those Fred Astaire and Ginger Rogers movies," Winnie said, breaking into Faith's thoughts. She was pounding nails into a huge Colin's House danceathon banner. "You know, the ones where Fred and Ginger are just an ordinary couple who suddenly become all the rage on the dance floor. They dress to the nines and step out of limos, wearing furs and carrying little poodles."

Faith looked at her sharply. "Be careful, Winnie. You shouldn't be up there. You're in no condition to risk falling down."

"Faith." Winnie looked hurt. "I'm careful. What's wrong with you?"

"Nothing," Faith snapped. A knot was tightening in her stomach from too much coffee.

"Lighten up," Liza sang. "Winnie's fine."

"Liza?" Faith changed the subject. "Do you and

Kimberly have the logistics worked out on the contest?"

"Uh huh. We'll start with an hour of dance music, then begin the first contest, which is a rap number," Kimberly rattled off. "Then there'll be one contest after another. All the winners will be announced around eleven. Then we'll play music for another two hours, until closing time."

"Good." Faith nodded. "And you're still going to emcee?"

"Absolutely," Kimberly answered. "Can you believe that we've sold more than four hundred advance tickets at ten dollars a pop? That's four thousand dollars so far."

Merideth got up from behind the bar, heaving a tank of soda concentrate. "We'll get at least as much as that in last-minute sales."

Robert was nodding. "And the contest-entry fees will be just gravy."

"Good," Faith answered faintly, slipping into a folding chair and reaching for her can of soda. Thoughts came into her mind, some painful, some happy.

She watched her friends, her eyes feeling like two heavy rocks in her head. Everyone seemed so joyful and alive. Danny Markam was rocking his wheelchair back and forth to a rap tune someone had slipped into the CD player. Liza was doing a tap dance in the middle of the floor. Kimberly was rushing around with a clipboard and Melissa was hobbling around with a stack of CDs.

Would she be able to muster exuberance by tonight? Faith wondered.

"This place looks great," Merideth was murmuring into her ear.

Faith jumped and looked back. "Yes—yes it does."

"You okay?"

"Yeah," Faith said hoarsely. "I just need some air. I'll be right back."

Faith's chair tumbled behind her as she tore out of the building and onto the sidewalk. She found a spot under the club's hot-pink awning where she could watch the streets quieting after the late-afternoon shopping rush. Across the way the windows of a department store darkened, and a delivery van rumbled into a nearby alley. Two noisy teenage guys in sloppy sweatshirts skateboarded by.

Faith felt her chest quaking. Then she felt the tears flooding her eyes. There was no holding back now. Sick at heart, she covered her face and felt the wetness between her fingers. How long would Merideth survive? Was there a chance he'd stay healthy long enough for someone to find a cure? Or would he end up like Casey—dying in a hospice, too weak to think or eat or care. It was too terrible to think about.

Boom, boom, boom, ba-boom, baboom boom. Boom, boom, boom, ba-boom baboom boom.

Faith looked up as a green car passed slowly by.

She cringed, wiping her cheek absently with the back of her hand. A bunch of tough-looking guys in army jackets leered at her through the car's open windows.

Faith stood up and started to go in, but noticed that the car was cruising back toward her again. The guys looked like they had shaved heads and they were jerking their bodies to the beat of the heavy-metal music.

As the car drew near to the club, it suddenly slowed.

Faith gulped. She stared at the guy behind the wheel and drew back. His smile made her blood run cold.

Were they planning to buy tickets to the danceathon? Faith hoped not. Of course, the danceathon was open to the public, but what if a bunch of thugs like that joined in? There might be trouble. Big trouble. Even violence.

Faith racked her brain. She stood up and hugged herself against the cool air. She could call the police and ask them to keep an eye out. But if she did that, they might end up disrupting the dance and turning off ticket-buyers.

The danceathon had to be a success. She was doing it for Merideth.

And she wasn't going to let *anyone* ruin this night.

Dash snapped shut his worn paperback copy of

The Maltese Falcon and flung it against his apartment wall. He sprang to his feet, crossed his arms, and began pacing his small room like an animal in a cage.

As usual, his sagging bookshelf was littered with coffee cups and balled-up papers. As usual, his typewriter was an island in the middle of half-written columns, day-old sandwiches, and piles of government documents.

He couldn't stand it anymore. He had to get out. He had to do something to prove his innocence. Sure, Lauren was trying to help. She was doing her best to track down Billy Jones and his gang.

But how far could she get, writing for a slick women's magazine? And even if she did get something published, how long would it take? Would the authorities follow it up? By that time, he could be formally charged with firebombing the Tri Beta house. By that time, he might be buried so far into the state penitentiary no one would ever find him.

Dash let out a sharp breath, yanked open his desk drawer, and pulled out a crushed pack of cigarettes. Slipping the last cigarette between his lips, he dug around for a book of matches and lit up.

"Saturday night," he muttered to himself. "Saturday night and there's nothing I can do. They've got me." He pounded his fist into the wall.

Bang. Bang. Bang, Dash heard the woman below banging a complaint on her ceiling.

Throwing himself into his desk chair, Dash took another drag of his cigarette and tried to settle down. When his dad bailed him out of jail earlier that week, the police had warned him to be on his best behavior and lie low.

"What the hell," Dash suddenly said, his eyes drifting miserably out the window. "What have I got to lose, anyway? They've probably already written up the charges. Assault with a deadly weapon. Arson. Malicious mischief. I'll be spending the next ten years in jail for my so-called attack on the Tri Beta house. I might as well enjoy life while I can."

Just then, Dash spotted a catchy ad on the back of the latest U of S *Weekly Journal*. He grabbed the copy and read it.

DANCEATHON. HELP SUPPORT SPRING-FIELD'S ONLY AIDS HOSPICE. *Dance your heart out. Sing your lungs out! Saturday, 8 p.m., The Glass Slipper. $10 admission.*

Dash stood up, taking one last deep drag of his cigarette, then ground it into his ashtray. A lot of loud, crazy music was just what he needed right now. And he might as well party while he could.

It might be the last party he'd go to in a long, long time.

Dash paused for a moment. He knew that Hearly had been tailing him for the last few days. But he didn't care anymore. Yanking his door open, Dash pounded down the staircase and out to his '67 Chevy. There wasn't one minute of freedom to waste. Quickly, he started the engine and looked around for any sign of Hearly. No cop was in sight.

So Dash, his mind jumping, his muscles twitching, gripped the steering wheel and headed to The Glass Slipper.

He was going to dance until he his mind was completely numb.

It was ten P.M. when he made his way through the huge crowd of students packed beneath the club's pink awning. Music was throbbing steadily out of the door. Laughter was floating in the air.

Inside the club, everything was dark and packed with bodies. Dash could barely see. He slapped down his money, and a burly guy stamped his hand with a fluorescent pass. Lights flashed and glittered. Streamers slipped playfully over his face. A Jimi Hendrix guitar riff was blasting out of the sound system, and Dash could feel his mind let go.

"DAAASH!" a foghornlike voice blared as he began to shoulder his way through the crowd. *"HI!"*

Dash felt a hand on his shoulder and turned around. It was Liza. He smiled, feeling carefree for once. Liza was usually the last person in the world he wanted to run into. But now he looked at her fire-engine-red lips and her skintight, gold lamé, off-the-shoulder dress as if she were a piece of candy that had dropped in his lap.

"Let's dance," Dash said, grabbing Liza around her ample waist and drawing her onto the dance floor.

"Ahhhh!" Liza screamed with delight as he took

her hand and threw her back into a wild arc. Her painted toenails flashed, and her white skin shone in the wild light. "I've always had a thing for you, Dash," Liza confessed loudly as she kicked her heels up.

"You tore your dress," Dash yelled as Liza continued to dance.

"So what?" Liza laughed, blowing him a kiss. "I needed a little air anyway."

After a while, Liza peeled herself away to dance with Merideth. But Dash was barely conscious of it. The music pounded and groaned in his ears. The darkness wrapped around him like a blanket. There was no yesterday, no tomorrow, no ugly skinheads and no pigheaded cops. Just the music and the lights and the darkness and the heat.

"I'm an animal!" Dash shouted crazily against the music. "Come and get me! Put me back in the cage. See if I care!"

"Yoo-hoo! Dash!" he heard someone yell in his ear. For a brief moment he thought it might be Lauren. But when he twirled around, he saw that it was only Winnie, dressed in a man-size black T-shirt emblazoned with a huge peace sign made out of neon-green sequins.

"Hey." He tried not to frown. His eyes began roaming the crowd, now anxious for a sign of Lauren.

"Hey yourself," Winnie yelled, bopping up and down to an old sixties tune. "Have you seen Josh?"

"Nope."

"He's got a job!" Winnie shouted happily. "With this really straight law firm that's making him wear a tie. And he's making tons of money. Can you believe it?"

"Great," Dash yelled back. Nothing surprised him anymore. Josh Gaffey selling out and wearing a tie. Liza Ruff with her underwear in plain sight. The next thing he knew, Lauren would be prancing in here with a rose between her teeth, begging him to run away with her.

If only it were true. But it wasn't. Things weren't that easy. Or fair. You try to love someone. You try to protect people like the Tri Betas from a bunch of murdering Nazis. And you get your head kicked in. There was no justice. No sanity.

Maybe it's time for me to leave the country, he thought.

Dash stopped bouncing and flailing for a minute. On a corner of the dance floor, he saw Kimberly.

"Kimberly!" Dash shouted, bouncing toward the edge of the jam-packed dance floor. Beautiful, tall Kimberly was dressed in a mod sixties minidress— her long, dark legs rising up out of a pair of white go-go boots. "Have you seen Lauren?"

"Nuh-uh." Kimberly shook her head, breaking into a dance that looked as if she were treading water in a sea of bodies. "Haven't seen her all night," she yelled back.

"Where are you, Lauren?" Dash mumbled to himself, falling back into the writhing crowd and wondering if she was the only thing left in his life worth sticking around for. How much more could he take? The skinheads and the bigots and creeps were taking over the world, while reporters like himself were getting silenced.

Where is she, anyway? Dash began to worry. He knew she was following Billy Jones's trail. Had she found something? Was she being careful? Did she know how dangerous these guys were?

Did anyone understand? Dash thought desperately as he whirled his head to the music and lost himself in the sound of the drum and the screaming guitars.

Fourteen

"**D**efendants request that, pursuant to RCW 4. 28. 360, the plaintiff set forth the amount claimed for each and every item of special damages and the amount of general damages sought in the complaint served in this matter. Such request shall be answered within fifteen days of service herein . . ."

Josh crashed his fist down on the tape recorder's OFF button. Then he looked up and stared at the sterile gray computer in front of him.

"What in the hell are these people talking about?" he asked the screen, shoving his hands into his pockets. He stuck his legs out in front of him and shoved his back against his chair.

It was Saturday night. For the last eight hours, he'd been taking dictation from a disembodied, droning voice inside the tape machine. He was beginning to imagine his brain as a long gray treadmill. Words went in through his ears, then came out through his fingers into the computer.

Tap, tap, tap, tap, bang. Josh began typing furiously. A stream of icy air blasted down from the air-conditioning vent in the ceiling.

You bet you're damaged by the guy who accidentally hit you and sprained your neck, Josh began entering a reply to the accident victim into the computer.

You're brain damaged. You want to get paid for pain and suffering and emotional distress on top of your medical bills? Hey, maybe I should sue someone for all my pain and distress since Winnie got pregnant. Then we'd have money. Maybe I should sue Winnie herself. She's the one who forgot the birth control that one afternoon.

Josh shivered and rubbed his temples. The countless cups of coffee he'd drunk were making his head buzz. Suddenly the gray walls had a funny texture to them, the computer keyboard was full of unfamiliar smudges, the small clock in the corner of the desk was without numbers. Josh squinted. Had the long hand moved a fraction of an inch? Or had time stopped?

Pushing back his office chair, Josh stood up abruptly, sucking in air. His metal garbage can overturned. He jumped, gun-shy, at the first sound he'd heard in hours. His high-school-graduation tie pinched his neck like a noose. He was ready to strangle all lawyers.

"What am I doing?" Josh muttered to himself, sitting back weakly in the chair. He looked at his watch.

Eight forty-five P.M.

"I've worked nearly eight hours at nine dollars per hour," Josh whispered miserably to himself. "That's seventy-two dollars, minus maybe twelve dollars in taxes. That's sixty bucks. Three weeks' worth of diapers."

Josh rubbed his sore eyes and looked at the computer. He clicked his ballpoint pen nervously and tried to steady his breathing.

Before today, he had loved all computers. The new ones. The old ones. The funky ones. Even the big, clunky ones that no one knew how to operate. Because he could always make them work. Before today, he could easily spend eight hours in front of a screen. That's where he thought he belonged. It was his life.

Until today.

Today he hated computers. Josh banged the tape recorder, accidentally pushing the ON button.

"Defendants above-named, by and through their attorneys of record, Hoskins, Stempler, and Bremen, request the Court to reschedule the . . ."

"Agggghhhhh!" Josh cried out, turning off the machine and very nearly throwing it against the wall. The computer manuals on the shelf above him spilled over to the side, and one dropped on top of his hands.

I'm locked in a prison with a lifetime sentence, while Winnie is hanging out at a disco party! Josh fumed. *I'm going to lose my soul and my spirit and my youth trying to meet my obligations, while Winnie is out playing Party Mom!*

In a white-hot instant of rage, Josh ripped off his jacket, pulled off his tie, and switched off the computer. Then, with shaking hands, he pulled out a plain sheet of paper from the steel desk and scrawled, I QUIT.

Storming down the sterile hallway, Josh passed a row of empty offices and glared at the abstract paintings in the huge reception area. He ducked into a small metal security door that slammed shut behind him, and he was suddenly, blissfully in the fresh, cool air.

Josh hugged his motorcycle helmet under his arm and looked back at the dark building with its slick, black front and glass doors.

"You're not going to suck me in," Josh muttered, turning away and gazing in the direction of the green mountains that swept up from Springfield Valley to the east of the campus. It was the open road he needed right now. He knew Winnie wanted to meet him at the danceathon, but there was no way he was going to go.

The only thing he wanted was to ride into the big black sky.

Josh turned and hurried to the side of the building, where his shiny motorcycle stood waiting for him like a life preserver. He buckled his helmet onto his head, lifted one leg, gunned the engine, and gripped the wide-spaced handlebars. His head suddenly free and light, he pushed off and sped out onto the downtown Springfield boulevard that eventually led to the foothills.

His eyes were fixed on the beam of his single headlight, and as he leaned into the first turn up into the mountains, he knew he'd done the right thing.

He and Winnie needed money for their baby.

But there had to be another way.

There just had to be.

KC's heart was racing.

The KRUS deejay's booth was dimly lit, and the volume was low as a long cut played lazily into the night.

"Mmm," Cody breathed. "Saturday night and no one's here."

Cody had lifted her onto his lap and was running his long fingers slowly through her dark hair. KC's head fell back a little as his lips dropped down to hers and his arms wound around her tightly.

After that morning's Tri Beta battle over Courtney, KC had left Annie and raced through campus to KRUS, where she had found Cody and spent most of the day planning his show for that night.

KC felt wonderfully warm. "Everyone's at the danceathon."

"Right," Cody murmured back, leaning down to brush her bare neck with his lips. Little shivers sank through KC's body. Even after spending practically the whole day together, she still couldn't get enough of him.

"Five more minutes," he whispered, "and we can leave."

"Okay." KC tickled his ear, then trailed her fingers down his bare neck until she could see the goose bumps rising on his skin. She could have stayed there all night. Time was shadowy. The world was shrinking away. There was just the two of them in this small circle of light. Only this closeness. Only this feeling of skin and touch and movement and longing.

"I love you." Cody gazed down at her, his eyes deep, holding her steady.

"Let's not go to the dance, then," KC said, looking steadily back at him, running her hand down the front of his soft white shirt. "Let's just go back to my room—or yours."

Cody nuzzled KC's ear. "Have I ever told you how much I like the shape of your ear?"

"You're changing the subject," KC reminded him, sitting up and looking at him carefully.

"Yes, well . . ." Cody's eyes shifted over to the door. "I think I'd better change the subject. The next deejay has arrived." He reached across her to his KRUS playlist on the control-board counter. "We're going to have to finish this later."

KC pulled back, making herself wake up. "I'll wait outside."

She waved Cody's replacement into the studio and headed out to the waiting room, collapsing next to a stack of year-old subscription magazines and coffee-stained newspapers. Then she turned and stared at Cody through the soundproof glass.

"Why are you the one I love?" KC asked softly, twisting the end of a lock of hair, knowing he couldn't hear. "Why are you the one I want to spend the whole night with? Why you? Why now? Why do I think I'm going to explode any second, just because we're separated by a few feet? A sheet of glass?"

Everything was different, KC realized. She'd crossed an invisible line, and now everything was very focused, very new, and moving very fast. It would have been a scary feeling, almost, if it hadn't been Cody. But it was Cody. And so it was as if she could pour all of her energy and trust and heart into something—someone—and know that it would be kept safe.

Maybe she was putting her life into someone else's hands. But it didn't matter anymore. She wasn't afraid.

"Okay." Cody shut the door to the studio behind him. "Let's get out of here."

KC stood up, slung her sweater over her shoulder, and fell into step with him as they left the station and made their way outside.

"Annie should be waiting for us," KC reminded him. "She really wanted to go to the danceathon."

"Good." Cody looked down into her eyes. "I like Annie. I like her attitude. She's open. She doesn't push stuff away. She takes it in."

"You're right," KC agreed, walking slowly back to Langston House, past Mill Pond and the University Theater and the skaters winding their way through the dark campus. KC tugged him closer around the waist as she stared out at the hundreds of tiny lights shining from the dorms. "I like her too."

There was a moment of silence as KC smiled to herself, just listening to her heels click along the pavement. All the thinking and planning and wondering was over. She just wanted to hold Cody and dance with him and spend the rest of the night with him. It was like powerful music that was pulling her along, and she wanted it never to stop.

She dragged Cody up the Langston House porch steps. "Let's see if Annie's ready." She darted up the stairs as Cody began to chase her. By the time they reached the end of the hallway, they were out of breath.

"Stop!" KC protested as Cody tried to pick her up. In one last desperate move, she slipped her key in the door and tumbled into the tiny room.

Then KC stopped.

The room was dark.

Carefully KC flicked on the light, and in the harsh overhead glare, she saw Annie, lying on the cot, staring at the ceiling.

KC took a step forward. "Annie?" she said softly.

She stared at Annie's blank face. It was pale, as if it had been drained of all blood. Her freckles stood out like angry specks, and her eyes were rimmed with red. Her hands were laced over her chest. She was still the same person wearing the same batik blouse and skirt she'd worn that morning, but there was something very different about Annie right now. Something had happened.

"Yes?" Annie barely whispered.

KC took another few steps forward and narrowed her eyes. She looked around the room. Everything was still in place. Annie's suitcases. Her art portfolio hanging from the closet door. Her stacks of art books on the floor, and the neat row of organic lotions on the dresser.

Then KC noticed that Annie was holding something. On her chest, pinned beneath her interlaced fingers, were a few folded pieces of paper that looked like letters or information sheets.

"Annie?"

KC cast a terrified look over her shoulder at Cody, who stood quietly at the door. Then she knelt down next to her friend. "Has something happened?"

Annie's face was a white stone.

"Annie?" KC tried again. "Annie, what are you holding?"

KC watched as Annie gripped the papers tighter,

until they crunched under her knuckles. Then she remembered: Annie had been hoping to hear about an art internship in Rome. She must have gotten the letter today—they must have turned her down.

"Please go," Annie said in a barely audible whisper.

"No," KC protested. Somehow, the pallor on Annie's face reminded her of her own, so many months ago, when she had lost her father. Just looking at Annie made the old feelings sweep over her like a wave. "I won't leave you this way."

"You can't help."

"Not if you don't tell me what's wrong," KC said, trying to balance herself between her bed and the narrow cot. "Listen, Annie. I know how bad things can get. I mean, if it's anyone in your family . . . I—I just lost my father. I—"

"It's not that," Annie said quietly, not looking at her. Her eyes were like two dark bruises. "Please. I can't talk."

Cody stirred at the door. "Listen, you two. I'm going to take off. Don't let me—"

"No," Annie said, turning over, exhausted. From the look of the creases in her clothes, KC realized that she'd been lying there for hours. The back of her hair was a ratty bird's nest. "You both go."

"Come on." KC put her hand on Annie's shoulder. "Why don't you come with us? We're going to the danceathon, remember? Maybe it'll take your mind off whatever's bothering you. Go with us."

"No!" Annie said suddenly, loudly.

"Annie." KC drew back, startled. "I don't understand."

Annie sat up, wobbled a little, and tried to wipe her cheek with her hand. There were red splotches all over her fair skin, and her lips were cracked and bluish. "I'm not going with you to the dance. I'm not going anywhere."

"What?"

"Not to the dance," Annie said shakily. "Not to Europe. Not to grad school. Not to the great museums . . . Nowhere. So get out. Just get out and have fun while you can."

KC stared in horror as Annie sat, looking straight ahead, not seeing.

"If you're having financial problems," KC tried again, desperate, "I know about that too. . . ."

"KC," Cody warned, placing a hand on her shoulder.

"Are you mad at me?" KC asked tearfully, too upset to think straight. "Did I mess up with Courtney? Is that it?"

Annie set her jaw and shook her head, continuing to stare as if she were mesmerized by the thumbtacks on KC's bulletin board. "Please," she whispered.

"I'm not going to leave!" KC suddenly burst out. "You're scaring me, Annie. It's not fair."

"KC—stop!" Cody said.

"That's right. Stop badgering me," Annie

screamed, holding two shaking fists in front of her. Her eyes were on fire in her pale, hollow face, and her wild red hair stuck out all around her head like a madwoman's.

KC drew back, collapsing on her bed. She watched, terrified, as Cody leaned over to say something low to Annie, but as he did, Annie pushed him away, grabbed a sweater off her bed, and ran sobbing out of the room.

"Annie!" Cody called out down the hall. "Wait."

KC jumped up and ran past him.

But by the time she reached the main entrance, all she could see was Annie's slight figure running across the dorm green, her white sweater flapping like a cry for help in the darkness.

Fifteen

"The car still there?" Jamie whispered, tense.

"Yeah," Lauren breathed, peering nervously around the corner of the alley. She and Jamie were watching the skinheads' car, which was parked across the street from The Glass Slipper. "They're just sitting there, smoking cigarettes and staring."

"Damn."

"Yeah." A trickle of perspiration started down the side of Lauren's cheek. Her mouth was dry and her throat was throbbing so hard with fear that she could barely talk. If they were right about Billy Jones's plan to harass the AIDS fund-raiser, things were sure to get bad—and soon. She'd never felt so

scared and helpless in her life. "We can't get the police in here unless they actually *do* something."

Jamie leaned up against the wall. His hair was di-
sheveled and his natty dress shirt was covered with
dirt. Since overhearing the skinheads' plans the night
before at the bowling alley, the two of them had been
following the group's movements, hoping to uncover
some concrete evidence they could give the police.

"Now I think we should just have told the cops
what we knew," Jamie whispered, disgusted. "If
these guys hate gays as much as they hate blacks,
we're in for a bloodbath."

"Oh, my God," Lauren moaned, jerking her
head back. "They're getting out of the car."

She flattened herself against the wall again and
slipped as close to the corner as she could, straining
to hear.

". . . ing queers . . . worse than the foreigners
taking over . . ." Lauren could hear Billy Jones's
high-pitched sneer. She stuck her head out for a second and watched as he slung his wiry leg around the
front of his car. Then he positioned his boot on the
front fender, crossed his arms, and gave the Glass
Slipper entrance a menacing glare.

Lauren remained in place. She and Jamie were
behind Billy now, and sunk back far enough into the
shadows to remain unseen. A few cars whizzed by,
and a burst of laughter rang out into the street. She
heard a car door open and clenched her teeth as a
second gang member emerged from the green sta-

tion wagon on their side of the street, his eyes darting up and down. "Two of them are out of the car now," Lauren whispered back over her shoulder. She narrowed her eyes. It was the guy with the tattoo, wearing the same sleeveless black jacket.

Jamie pulled Lauren back and slowly edged around the corner for a view. "These guys are such lowlifes," he whispered angrily as he ducked back. "They make me want to—"

"Stay down!" Lauren snapped. "Look."

"Oh, no," Jamie moaned.

Together they watched, sick at heart, as two guys strolled away from the dozen or so people crowded outside the danceathon. Even from her position across the street, Lauren could clearly see that they were partners. And one of them was Faith's close friend, Merideth Paxton.

Lauren's eyes darted between Merideth and Billy Jones.

A chill went through her body. Merideth was putting his arm around the other guy's shoulder. Billy had obviously noticed them. But Merideth and his friend were completely oblivious to the gang around the green car.

"What's happening?" Jamie tugged her backward. Lauren pulled him forward, but kept her head ducked down. The skinheads weren't going to notice them now. They wanted Merideth and his friend. They wanted to ruin the Glass Slipper fund-raiser.

Billy's fist was pounding loudly on the car hood

and he was motioning his head toward Merideth and Robert, who were now strolling back toward The Glass Slipper's pink awning. The guy with the tattoo nodded and punched one fist into the palm of his other hand.

"Get 'em. Get 'em, Mack, so they don't forget," Billy ordered.

Lauren panicked. "Jamie! What do we do?"

". . . ing faggots," Lauren could hear Mack answering back as he waited for a car to pass, then began walking slowly across the street, pounding his fist and cracking his knuckles.

Lauren glanced over at the small group in front of the club. No one seemed to notice what was happening. It looked as if Merideth and his friend were going to get jumped any moment.

"I think I'll scream," Lauren whispered. "Anything to distract them. It'll give Merideth some time."

"No!" Jamie tried to stop her. "These guys are death."

"Are you morons ready in there?" Billy called out hoarsely to the others in the car. He was still positioned on the car hood, but looked as if he were ready to spring.

Lauren squinted. In the car's backseat, she could see three guys busily at work. She gasped. Could they be putting together the same gasoline-filled bottle bombs that had destroyed the Tri Beta house?

Lauren stared back at Mack, who had begun menacing Merideth.

Everyone, including those in front of the club, froze.

Meanwhile, the three remaining skinheads emerged from the backseat of the green station wagon, gasoline-filled bottles in hand.

"Oh no!" Lauren gasped, standing up. "Jamie, they're—"

"Stay back!" Jamie barked.

"Look out. They've got firebombs!" Lauren screamed, bursting out of the alley. It was too late. She didn't care. She couldn't hold back. Billy Jones swiveled around, jumped off the car hood, and faced her, his ugly teeth bared in the streetlight. The other gang members stood paralyzed in the middle of the street, waiting for a signal.

Lauren planted her feet and stared Billy Jones down. "Get out of here," she breathed.

Billy Jones smiled. "You want us to leave?" he teased.

Lauren shivered. She felt Jamie behind her, but she couldn't back off. These ugly, worthless thugs had spread hate and fear all over Springfield. They'd harassed Dash and nearly killed her friends at the Tri Beta house. She wasn't going to sit back and be afraid while people got hurt. Holding back her anger simply wasn't something she could do anymore.

And right now, she was prepared to do anything to save Dash from prison.

"Huh?" Billy's upper lip was curled into a threatening sneer. Quickly he looked back at the gang members in the street and motioned for them to proceed.

"What the hell do you think you're doing?" Lauren heard herself shout. She knew she was taking a huge risk with her life—and maybe with Jamie's, too. But at that moment, everything in her life fell away except her rage.

"Hey, little blond lady," Billy snickered. "We're here to save you from the foul elements in society." He took a step forward.

"Get away from her," Jamie growled behind Lauren. "Just stay away."

"Oh," Billy cooed. "Oh, hurt me. Hey, fellas. Did you hear the man? He wants us to go away. Maybe he's a faggot-lover too."

"Well, I sure got some fairies here," Mack shouted from across the street. "Isn't that right?"

Lauren drew in her breath, terrified, as Mack shoved Merideth. The group at the door shrank back inside. The three other thugs remained frozen next to the car, firebombs in hand, waiting for a signal from Billy. The street had suddenly become an elaborate chess game. Everyone was waiting to see who would make the next move.

"Go home, little woman," Billy said to Lauren. "That's where you belong—with your apron on."

"You're sick," Lauren shrieked as Jamie tried to pull her back.

"Yeah. You hate everyone because you hate *yourself*," Merideth shouted. He caught Mack's swinging fist in his hand and kicked Mack in the groin. "I feel sorry for you," he added, running toward Billy.

"Hah, you'll be feeling a lot more when I'm through with you and your *boy*friend."

"Get inside," Merideth yelled back to Robert as Mack started a shoving match. "Get help."

Billy's goons began to circle Lauren, Jamie, and Merideth. Lauren could see their shaved heads shining like grease in the streetlight.

"Cluck, cluck, cluck," Billy turned to taunt Merideth. "You get out of this town, little fairy-boy. You're contaminating the community."

Lauren glanced desperately over to the Glass Slipper entrance, hoping for reinforcement. The music had died down, and she could see that the windows had quieted. Closing her eyes, she prayed for help. She, Jamie, and Merideth were outnumbered. And the firebombs needed only a simple match.

"C'mere, queen," Billy taunted again. "You and the Jews, and niggers, and spics, and chinks and all other impure races deserve what you—"

There was a sudden noise as the door to The Glass Slipper was flung open. Amidst the commotion, Lauren saw a guy with scraggly dark hair and a leather jacket leap out onto the sidewalk.

"Hey!" the guy cried out. "They're over here."

Lauren's eyes opened wide. Her head was pounding with fear. "Dash," she screamed.

Suddenly, a large crowd began following Dash out onto the sidewalk. She watched as Dash scanned the street until his eyes locked on to hers.

For a moment he stood still, taking in the situation. Lauren, Jamie, and Merideth were still frozen in the middle of the quiet street, facing off all five of the skinheads. But Dash was being followed by a swelling number of students and professors pouring out of the danceathon. Within a few moments, hundreds of partygoers had swarmed into the dank street and were slowly surrounding the skinhead thugs.

"You—are—scum," Dash spat out, walking slowly toward Billy Jones, his eyes full of anger.

"Dash, no!" Lauren burst out. "They have the firebombs."

Dash halted.

"You don't scare us, spic," Billy taunted as the other gang members slowly held up their beer-bottle bombs. "How many fags are still in there?"

Out of the corner of her eye, Lauren thought she saw something bright and swirling in the distance. A bead of sweat trickled down the side of her face.

The swirling light was now accompanied by a siren.

Suddenly, the entire crowd turned. A squad car moved in.

"Hold it!" one of the officers called out as he shut off the siren and got out of the car.

Billy froze, then turned on his heels like a panicked animal. Instinctively, Lauren tore after him, but the surrounding crowd held Billy and his thugs in place. In a flash, Lauren could see Billy grab one of the homemade Molotov cocktails and lift up his arm to throw it into a window of The Glass Slipper.

"Stop!" Lauren yelled, lunging for Billy and grabbing him by the wrist. She felt a strong hand on her back and whirled around to see a uniformed cop lock his arm around Billy's neck. Lauren gasped with relief. It was Dash's arresting officer, Lyle Hearly. The guy who'd been trailing Dash.

Lauren stepped toward him. "We've been watching them."

Hearly's eyes lifted and focused on Lauren, confused. One of his arms was still around Billy, while the other held up the homemade bomb. Several other police cars drew up, sending a swarm of officers over the trapped thugs. Within seconds, all five were in handcuffs.

"She's been watching them—tracking them," Dash called out. "Check the bomb out."

Hearly turned around. "Okay, fella. Calm down."

Dash moved forward as the rest of the dance-athon partygoers crowded around to listen. "It's the same kind of bomb that was used on the Tri Beta house."

Hearly passed the gasoline-filled bottle over to another officer, who turned it over in his hands and nodded.

"These guys are white-supremacist nut cases who've been harassing this community," Lauren tried to explain.

"It's what I've been trying to tell you for the last

week," Dash broke in, his face white and ragged.

Hearly shrugged, taking the bottle back. "Maybe."

"There's no maybe," Dash blurted.

"We'll check it out," Hearly boomed as the red lights began to swirl again and one of the cars drove off. "Now get your butt back home and let us do our work."

"Right," Dash muttered, his eyes moving toward Lauren, grateful.

Lauren's eyes were suddenly flooding with tears of relief and exhaustion. She knew they had to believe Dash. She knew that Dash was safe now. Her knees were wobbly and her head felt faint, but just as she reached out to grab Dash, she felt another pair of strong arms wrap around her.

She didn't have to turn around to see who it was. She knew it was Jamie.

Three hours later, The Glass Slipper looked like a tornado had blown in from a nearby party-favor factory. Silver streamers were strewn gaily over the dance floor and tables. Balloons bounced listlessly underfoot. Sparkly confetti glittered in the tired hairdos of the few remaining partygoers, gathered in quiet groups near the door.

Faith sat alone on a chair, fiddling with a single rose she'd found on the floor. The danceathon had been a huge success. Even the excitement over the skinheads in the street hadn't dampened many spirits. After the police left, most of the people had returned for another two hours of dancing.

"Faith?" Merideth was calling her from the tiny office just off the main floor.

Faith rose, her face numb. Her ears were still ringing from the music, and she still didn't know how to tell Merideth that she knew he was ill.

"What's up?" she asked. "Good news?"

"Yes," Merideth muttered, punching numbers into a calculator. "Great news. The danceathon brought in more than nine thousand dollars."

"Nine thousand?" Faith's eyes opened wide. "I didn't know that many people came."

"It's a big hall," Merideth said with satisfaction. "Everyone came. It was a blowout."

Faith rose and wrapped her arms around Merideth's neck from behind. "We really did it."

Merideth looked back at her, his brown eyes glowing. "I can't wait to tell the folks over at Colin's House. It's going to mean so much."

"I know."

"It's not just the money for more nurses and more educational outreach," Merideth said quietly. "It's the fact that so many people showed that they cared."

"They do," Faith said softly, her eyes slowly filling with tears. How could he be so unselfish? He was facing the prospect of having AIDS himself, and all he wanted to do was help others.

"I mean, look at the way everyone rallied around us when those neo-Nazis showed up and threatened me," Merideth went on. "It wasn't just a dance to raise money. It was something more. I think when those skinheads showed up, a lot of people realized that there was more at stake than just protecting me from a bunch of goons."

Faith slipped her hand into his, part of her wanting to push away her thoughts about Merideth's real condition. It was tempting to pretend you could just fall back in time. Before AIDS. Before Merideth tested positive for the HIV virus. Back when everything in her life was innocent and free and light. But she couldn't go back. "Tell me."

Merideth bit his lip. "It was about the right to be who you are. It was about freedom and the right to choose the way you live."

Faith nodded. "Tolerance."

"Exactly. You know, I've been harassed like that before. People have called me all kinds of horrible things. But I don't sit back and take it anymore. I'm gay. It's not a choice, as much as it's just the way it is. And I have the right to tell the truth about myself and not get my head kicked in for it."

"Merideth . . ." Faith began. She knew she had to tell him what she knew. She had to be brave.

"That's why this fund-raiser was so important to me, Faith," Merideth went on softly. "It was about not sitting around and playing the victim. I can't do that anymore. Not if I can help it."

Faith put her other hand on top of the hand that was still holding his. Her heart was thumping, but she knew she had to speak now. "I—I think I know what you mean, Merideth. I mean, I think I know why you've been so upbeat today. You don't want to give in or be the victim. Even though, in a way, you are."

"What?" Merideth was staring at her, confused.

Faith looked at him, struggling for control, though her body was shivering and her hands were beginning to shake. "I know about the test result. I overheard you on the phone at Colin's House yesterday. The HIV . . . positive . . . result."

Merideth turned sharply in his chair and looked quizzically into her eyes. His dark eyebrows were narrowed and his goofy face was drained of all humor. "What are you talking about, Faith? Me? HIV positive?"

Faith drew in her breath sharply. "You're not . . . ?" she cried out. "But I thought for sure . . ."

Merideth was shaking his head in wonder. "The test came back negative. This morning, in fact. Robert's okay too. You mean . . . you thought all this . . . ?"

Something stuck in Faith's throat. It was as if the dam had been broken inside of her and a torrent had begun to flow outward. She could barely speak. "You're—not?"

"No, Faith," Merideth said softly. "No, I'm not."

Faith began to cry. Together they stood, slipping their arms around each other. Long, terrible sobs began to pour out of her, and it wasn't until then that she realized how much she had been holding in.

Grabbing her shoulders, Merideth pulled her away a little so that he could see her face. "We got some bad news about a friend of ours yesterday," he explained. "A really good friend. And we were—well, it was awful."

"Thank God," Faith cried.

"I'm okay," he repeated.

"And I'm not going to get the virus—ever," he said firmly. "I'm playing it safe, Faith. I stay protected. I value my life, and I value the people I love. I'm just not going to make any dangerous choices."

"I'm so relieved," Faith sniffed, clinging to Merideth as if she never wanted to let him go. "I can't tell you."

"I know," he murmured. "So was I."

"It's all so crazy," Faith said through her tears. "AIDS is so terrible and unfair."

"I know," Merideth said. "But listen. Getting that result didn't take anything away from the way I feel about this disease and the people who suffer and die from it. I'm not going to walk away. I'm not going to turn my back on those who aren't as lucky as I am. It's just not going to be that way for me."

"Then I'm with you, Merideth," Faith said quietly. "I'm with you."

Sixteen

"Let's hurry."

"She's probably okay, KC."

"No, I'm worried, Cody. We should have come back earlier."

It was way past midnight, and the long walk home from The Glass Slipper had cleared KC's mind. Her head was cool. And her memory of Annie's ragged face was painfully sharp.

"Come on," KC urged Cody, leading him away from the campus pathway into a shortcut past Mill Pond. She yanked off her dance shoes and took in the cool feeling of the grass on her bare feet.

"Okay." Cody loped alongside her, his long, dark hair flying. "You might be right about Annie being in serious trouble. It's been quite a night. First those skinheads outside the disco, then all the suspense over whether Courtney would hand over that three thousand dollars to Colin's House . . ."

"Oh, she wouldn't have done it," KC protested. "The whole thing was ridiculous."

"Then you were out on the dance floor, taking on the sixties freestyle dance competition," Cody teased, holding up her imitation gold-leaf trophy of a dancing couple. "No one looked as wild as you, KC. I loved the way you sorta let your arms go limp and stared at the ceiling like a spaced-out groupie."

"My parents taught me all the moves," KC replied, lifting her skirt and jumping over a flower bed.

Up ahead, she could see Langston House, but the window of her dorm room was dark. "We should have chased Annie down," KC said worriedly. "Something bad happened."

"She didn't want you to know," Cody said. "On the other hand, the light could be off because she came back and went to sleep."

"I hope so," KC replied, turning into the Langston House pathway and running up the porch steps. Together, she and Cody took the stairway two steps at a time.

"Here goes," KC said nervously when they reached her door. She slipped in her key, unlocked it, and pushed open the door carefully. KC drew her breath in sharply. All she could see was the dim out-line of her neatly made bed and desk.

Annie's cot was empty.

"Annie?" KC said, hoping she was wrong. She fumbled for the overhead light and switched it on. All of Annie's suitcases, books, and art supplies stood quietly in place.

But Annie was definitely not there.

"It's one o'clock in the morning," KC breathed, setting down her trophy and raking her hair with her fingers. "Where could Annie be? I'm scared, Cody."

Cody paced, then stopped and stuffed his hands in the pockets of his leather vest. "Does she have any real close friends on campus?"

"Well, I'm not sure . . ."

"Any place she hangs out, or—"

KC clamped her hand to her forehead, whirling around in the tiny room. "Yes, the art studio," KC burst out, her mind suddenly flipping into gear. "She has some kind of hideout there! And she has a key, so she could be there now!"

Cody's eyes were blazing. "I'll go with you."

"No." KC was rummaging through the back of her closet, finally pulling out a pair of boots. "I'll call you at your place if I don't find her."

"If you don't find her, I'm calling campus security."

"Okay," KC shouted over her shoulder as she ran down the hall and into the night. She ran across the dewy dorm green toward the U of S art studios. She knew they were located somewhere behind the

Humanities Building, but she had no idea which one Annie went to.

Please, please, please, Annie. Please be there. Please let everything be okay, KC prayed. *Nothing in life can be as bad as it seems at the moment. Time heals a lot of things, Annie. Please give it time, whatever it is!*

KC's heart was thumping, and her long hair was tangled and sweaty by the time she reached a low group of deserted buildings at the edge of campus. Framed by a few scraggly cottonwoods, the arty-looking buildings had funky angles and large windows. But it was hard to see where the entrances were. Aside from a few lights along the pathway, it was pitch-black.

Not to the dance. Not to Europe. Not to grad school. Not to the great museums. Nowhere. Annie's words echoed in KC's mind.

"What was she talking about?" KC mumbled, gasping for breath, trying the front entrance door.

Locked.

KC's boots crunched on the gravel as she ran around to the side of the building. The night air was cool against her face, but inside, she was shaking with fear.

After trying all of the doors, KC staggered down the path toward a second group of buildings. In the distance, she thought she could see a small flicker of light through an angled skylight. Her fear began to boil into an angry determination.

KC ran around the second building, furiously yanking at door handles, banging, yelling, and calling Annie's name. She was breathing hard as she ran around to the back and spotted a blue door partly hidden behind a row of Dumpsters. She grabbed it and yanked, then nearly fell over.

It was open!

KC slipped inside a dark, eerie hallway, not knowing whether to move forward or run back to the safety of Cody's arms. Dim light filtered down through a row of high windows, and the bushy cottonwoods scratched spookily against the side of the building.

"Annie?" KC tried to call. She clamped her mouth shut, frustrated. Her throat was so tight, all that came out was a frightened squeak.

Slowly KC moved down the hallway. The cold air smelled like clay, and the darkness was beginning to suffocate her. All she could hope for was to find the light. It might be Annie, or someone who could tell her where she was. KC slowed, trembling. At the end of the hallway, a door was slightly ajar. She shivered. Light was definitely coming from inside. Why was she so scared?

"Annie?" she called out, this time louder. "Are you in there, Annie?"

KC stepped in quietly. It was a huge, high-ceilinged studio, scattered with easels, potter's wheels, half-finished sculptures, and huge canvases suspended from the ceiling. Long tables were haphazardly arranged, and the wooden floor was spattered with paint. Now she could see where the light was coming from. There was some kind of ledge in the corner of the studio.

KC gulped.

"Annie?" she whispered one more time. The room was so quiet and eerie, she couldn't stand it.

"I'm here," KC heard a small voice at the other end of the cavernous space.

"Annie?" KC spoke up, stepping ahead, her heart in her throat, half relieved, half terrified. Slowly, carefully, she walked across the deserted studio, gripping onto the sides of tables and columns to steady herself in the darkness.

Then she looked up and saw Annie. KC drew in her breath. A small couch had been set up on a platform a few feet above the studio floor, and a candle flickered on an overturned box in front of it. There, in the dim light, she could see Annie lying on her back, staring at the ceiling, her hair like a wild mane around her motionless face.

KC moved forward, her footsteps hollow against the wooden steps. "Please tell me." KC knelt down next to Annie. "You've got to," KC begged. "I can't bear it."

Slowly, Annie's eyes moved in KC's direction. For a moment, they hung sadly on KC's, then dropped down to the upside-down box in front of them, which was scattered with papers. "Take a look," she said faintly.

KC frowned. She reached down and picked up a light-blue pamphlet.

"'Q and A about HIV and AIDS,'" KC strained to read in the candlelight. "'Human Immunodeficiency Virus, or HIV, is a virus that attacks the body's immune system. Over time, the virus weakens a person's defenses against disease, leaving them vulnerable to many infections and cancers that would not normally develop in healthy people.'"

Annie was staring stone-faced at the flickering candle.

"What's this about, Annie?" KC mumbled, trying to think. "I don't understand."

KC shuffled frantically among the papers and pamphlets, finally pulling out a letter addressed to Annie—from the Red Cross Blood Center in Springfield.

Dear Ms. Neill, the letter read. *At the time of your recent blood donation, many routine screening tests were performed, one of which showed results outside the normal limits. Please call and make an appointment with us as soon as possible.*

KC froze.

Annie stirred and lifted her eyes up to KC. "Do you see now?" she asked quietly.

KC's mouth was falling open. Her throat was too tight to speak and her eyes were flooding. "What?" she cried out, panicked. "What is this?"

"Don't you remember this morning?" Annie whispered hoarsely. "The Red Cross called me back. The blood I donated two weeks ago. It didn't pass the screening test, KC. I have the HIV virus. The virus that causes AIDS."

"No!" KC cried, unable to move. *"NO!"*

Annie's shoulders were shaking now. Her face was beginning to collapse and her mouth was screwing up into a horrible, agonized shape. Suddenly, she was half sitting up, reaching out for KC's arms and sobbing. "Yes. Yes, it's true. They didn't want to call me up or just send me a letter. So they got me to come back, KC. And—and I—went in there—and there was a nurse waiting for me—and they took me into a room—and—and I was so scared, KC."

KC was gripping Annie tightly now. Her brain was numb and her heart was full of terror. Annie Neill? Nice girl Annie Neill? Sorority girl from a wealthy Seattle family?

With the HIV virus?

It was too horrible and strange for her to believe.

"They—they said," Annie began to talk through her sobs. "They said—that anyone can get it from—from having unprotected sex." Annie's body was collapsed over KC's lap now. "And I *did* go unprotected with that guy I met last summer in San Francisco, KC. I—I just didn't think about it."

"Oh, God, Annie," KC breathed.

"I didn't know a thing about him, KC. He—he popped into my life and all we knew was the present. We had dinner. We stared at each other. We fell into bed. We took long walks. We talked about art, KC. Not our health habits!"

"You—you didn't use condoms—ever?" KC asked gently.

Annie let out a bitter laugh. "I barely even knew what a condom was, KC. I use birth-control pills. It was never an issue!"

"Annie," KC said, trying to contain her emotions.

"How could I have been so stupid?" Annie screamed into the darkness.

KC's teeth chattered. She felt cold. This wasn't supposed to happen. People were supposed to want passion and love in their lives, weren't they? When did the penalty get so high?

"Annie," KC whispered. She felt a blackness sweep over them like a dark wing in the night. There was nothing she could say. Nothing she could do except let the truth sink in.

Annie sat up and hugged her arms to her chest. Fine blue circles surrounded her wet eyes. "I don't know know what to do. I don't know what comes next."

KC nodded. She thought about Cody. She thought about the random way things seemed to happen. People connected, or they didn't. There were survivors. And there were people who were cut off when they'd barely begun to live. Why one thing and not the other? Why Annie and not her? Why did KC love Cody, and not a man in San Francisco?

KC's lips parted a little as a desperate thought slipped through her. "Could it be a mistake?"

"No. I—I've always looked ahead, KC." Annie was whispering. "I can't get used to—not having that."

"You can. You will," KC whispered. "There'll be

time. You'll get to Europe. You'll see the paintings."

"Yes, but how much time?" Annie asked dully. "It's all about living in the present, KC. The moment right here and now is all there is."

KC looked over. "They may find a cure while you're still healthy."

"A cure," Annie repeated absently.

They have to, KC thought, making a fist and staring out over the half-finished sculptures that made shadows on the long walls beyond. *Why can't they? They've cured thousands of other diseases.*

"Maybe they will," Annie whispered back. Her cheek was wet against KC's shoulder. "But until they do, I'll be living my life with a sword. I don't know if I can cope with that."

"I know," KC said softly, wondering what had gone wrong with the world. It wasn't fair. Things were cruel. People were heartless. And there really was only the present. Why was that so hard to remember?

"I just don't know," Annie repeated as she and KC rocked slowly together on the couch, gripping each other in the darkness and staring at the half-finished art projects scattered below them in the fading candlelight.

Seventeen

"**O**ne quarter-cup serving of cottage cheese for seven to eight grams of protein," Winnie was reading hurriedly, nibbling on sunflower seeds and pressing the ON button on the blender.

It was Sunday morning in the kitchen of Winnie and Josh's off-campus bungalow, the day after the Colin's House dancethon. Winnie's eyelids were drooping and her head felt funny. But she was due at the hotline in a half hour—barely enough time to eat and walk.

"Winnie?" Josh glanced at her as he dragged through the kitchen door, wearing one of her Japanese kimonos which barely wrapped around his body. He wearily opened the fridge and pulled out a foil packet containing a leftover slice of pizza. Then he popped open a can of Coke, balanced the slice on top of it, and headed for the breakfast table.

"One three-ounce serving of broccoli—or cantaloupe—excellent daily Vitamin C source," Winnie was mumbling to herself as she poured her wheat germ–orange juice smoothie into a tall glass. "Plus raisins for iron and supplementary calories . . ."

"Winnie?" Josh repeated, sitting down with his breakfast, dragging the Sunday morning paper across the table. "Are you sure you're not mad?"

Winnie looked around, surprised. "Oh, hi. I'm just working out my prenatal diet for the day. No, I'm not mad. If you didn't like the law firm, you shouldn't have to work there. And I didn't even mind the fact that you rode your bike to Hauser Lake and back. It was probably good for you."

"Oh, okay." Josh bit into his pizza slice.

"I'm missing something from my whole-grains category," Winnie went on.

"Winnie?" Josh looked over his newspaper, his dark hair flopped over his tired eyes. "Don't you think you're taking this pregnancy diet a little too far?"

Winnie looked up slowly from her book, her mouth dropping open in disbelief. "What? Do you realize, Josh, that this is a critical time in the development of our baby's brain tissue and nervous system?"

Josh narrowed his eyebrows and took another mammoth bite. "Yeah. But bulgur wheat? Winnie, that quaint little health-food store charged you five dollars for that tiny little bag."

"It's important," Winnie said with finality, wondering when Josh was going to get with the program. They were going to be parents. Why was he having such a hard time remembering that? "Five dollars isn't that much, anyway."

Winnie stared as Josh's face hardened. "Five dollars is forty minutes' jail time at Hoskins, Bored and Heavy, after taxes, Winnie. That's what five dollars is."

"Well, thank goodness there will be no more jail time at that awful place, then," Winnie came back.

"Yes, but . . ."

"Actually, I'm quite relieved," Winnie said, taking a gulp of her frothy vitamin drink and settling down.

"Fine." Josh buried his head in the sports section.

Winnie sighed. There was no reason that making money and being miserable had to go hand-in-hand. She wiped the smoothie mustache off her mouth. "I hated the idea of you trapped in that stuffy office with that awful tie. You're too good for that."

Josh lowered the paper and gave her a quizzical look. "Too *good* for that? What do you mean? People have to do things they don't like all the time, especially when they're desperate for money."

Winnie stood up, placed her empty glass on the counter, and gazed down at the tiny mound on her stomach. *"BBBLLLUUUHHH."* She made a shuddering sound, shaking her head. "Don't talk that way,

Josh. We're not like that. We're smart. Educated. We're going to have fantastic jobs, doing what we love."

Josh rolled his eyes. "But we don't have our degrees, yet, Winnie. Don't you see? And we're looking at some grunt-work time for the next few years until we do. Aren't you worried about money?"

Winnie looked sorrowfully at Josh, plucked out the spikes in her hair, then slipped on a pair of orange-rimmed, wing-tipped sunglasses. She wished Josh would stop worrying so much. It was making her tense, and tension was bad for the fetus. "The money will come."

"But how, Winnie?" Josh began to argue.

Winnie thumped herself down on the chair opposite him. "Look, all this worrying about money is going to drive us apart, Josh Gaffey. We *will* find a way to earn extra money that doesn't turn us into a couple of automatons out of *Invasion of the Body Snatchers*. We're just going to have to give it a little more time. . . ."

"Time? There's no . . ."

"And I'm not going to have our baby growing up in a home with two parents who are miserable and brain-dead, simply because they were too stressed-out and unimaginative to think of fun ways to earn survival money," Winnie declared, turning to pace to the other end of the kitchen.

Josh popped his soda can open. "Body snatcher, huh?" He gulped his soda and chewed off a piece of cold pepperoni, staring at her.

Winnie planted her hands on her hips and glared at Josh in her bathrobe. Why was he always accusing her of acting like a little kid? He was the one who couldn't face facts. He was the one who quit his job after only one shift. Maybe she was the one who'd have to take charge.

"What are you staring at?" Josh growled, crumpling his newspaper and looking down at his hairy legs as if she'd spotted a strange insect.

"I have an idea."

"For what?"

"For money," Winnie said, stabbing a hot-pink nail into the side of her head.

"*You* are thinking about money?" Josh laughed softly into his paper.

"Yes, I am."

"What?"

Winnie crossed the kitchen floor and grabbed Josh's face between the palms of her hands until he looked at her. "The computer room."

"The computer room," Josh repeated, crossing his eyes.

"Yeah. Why don't we rent it out?"

Josh uncrossed his eyes. "Oh, you mean take on another roommate?"

"Well, that is, if Clifford and Rich don't mind," Winnie thought out loud. The computer room was really a bedroom in the off-campus bungalow she and Josh shared with their two friends. But now it was used for Josh's computer and extra storage for everyone else. "It would save us a hundred and fifty dollars a month."

"I don't know, Win," Josh warned. "We've got things working pretty smoothly around here right now. Throw another person into the equation, and you could have major trouble."

"Come on," Winnie insisted, grabbing her purse. She'd gone along with Josh's idea to work weekends. And now he'd have to give her idea a chance. "Let's talk to Rich and Clifford. After all, a penny saved is a penny earned."

"Okay," Josh mumbled, kissing her good-bye as she slung her purse over her shoulder and headed for the front door.

Winnie pulled open the door, then leaned back and gave Josh an irritated look. "After all, Josh. Pretty soon, we're *always* going to have an extra person tagging along. We might as well get used to the idea now."

Put, put, put, put, put, put, put, put.

Lauren's printer spit out the last page of her article on white-supremacist hate groups in small-town Springfield. She seized the sheet and grabbed the clock on her dorm desk.

Monday. Four o'clock. Still time to turn it in to *West Coast Woman*.

Lauren pushed her wispy hair off her face and stared at the finished piece. Since Saturday night's skinhead bust in front of The Glass Slipper, she'd been working on it nonstop. It had been a furiously fast effort, and she'd barely slept in two days.

And now it was done.

Yanking open her desk drawer, she pulled out a file folder and stuffed the piece inside. She rubbed her eyes. She shuddered. Saturday night seemed like a dream now. But a few details stuck in her mind she knew she'd never forget. The awful stillness in the street as she faced off with Billy Jones. The horrible, wild sneer on his face. The sight of the gasoline bombs. And then Dash.

Dash safe at last.

Tucking her black T-shirt into a pair of baggy pants, Lauren slipped into her shoes, scooped up her article, and headed for *West Coast Woman.*

She bit her lip as she headed out the main Forest Hall door. She'd left with Jamie on Saturday night. But it was Dash she'd wanted to talk to. He'd left for home after talking to the police, and she hadn't been able to reach him since. Lauren shook her head, hurrying across the dorm green toward the edge of campus. The afternoon sun was hot and the Mill Pond was crowded with sunbathers.

She headed down Springfield's main street, past the IceBurg, the Wagon Wheel dime store, and a group of high-school students playing classical music on the brick plaza of The Strand shopping area.

I need to talk to Dash now, not Jamie, Lauren suddenly realized, pushing open the now-familiar glass doors to the magazine office. *I should have mailed this in*.

Lauren looked out over the magazine's newsroom. Dash was practically the reason she'd become a writer. Last fall, she barely had enough nerve to submit a fluff piece to the campus paper. Now, thanks to Dash's encouragement and his tip about the *West Coast Woman* internship, she was tracking down dangerous hate-crime criminals in the street and living to tell the story for a prestigious national publication.

"Hi, Lauren," one of the staffers called out briskly. "He's in there ranting again."

"Okay," Lauren replied, almost wishing no one had seen her. She wanted to run back down to the street and hurry back to campus. She wanted to find Dash. Instead, she marched down the hall toward Jamie's office. She looked inside. He had just finished slamming down the telephone and was rubbing his face with his two propped-up hands.

"First draft." Lauren slapped the article down in front of him. "Three thousand words."

Jamie looked up, his eyes widening. His sixties-nostalgia tie was loose and his eyes had dark, tired circles underneath. "Already?"

Lauren shrugged. "It's rough. But I had to get it out of my system, I guess."

Jamie looked impressed. He slid the paper-clipped stack of copy across the table and turned it around so that it faced him. "Fast work."

"Well," Lauren said with a sigh, flopping down in

a chair, stuffing her hands into her front pockets, and sticking her legs out straight in front of her, "it would be nice to see it in print, if it ever gets that far."

Jamie's eyes were intently scanning the first page of the article. "It will be. It will be," he murmured, still reading. "Great lead. Looks like it's in great shape so far. Hey. Who taught you how to write like this?"

Lauren pressed her lips together, thinking of Dash. "I've had some good editors. One in particular," she added softly.

"Yeah, well, that—uh—always helps," Jamie said thoughtfully, not taking his eyes off her. He leaned back in his designer chair and laced his fingers lazily behind his head. There was something about his dark beard and inviting brown eyes that sent a warm thread of fascination through her. "There is one . . . thing . . . that could hold up publication of this story, though."

Lauren shifted. Jamie's flashing eyes were intense and his jaw was clenched beneath his dark beard. "What?"

Jamie sat up straight, planted his elbows on the desk in front of him, and looked down, embarrassed. "To keep you on staff longer."

"What?"

He shook his head. "Oh, never mind. I'm not really serious. It's just that since your internship involves only one story—it would be tempting to tell you that your story needed more work. That way I could work with you on it for another month and . . ."

"Another month?"

"Forget it, Lauren," Jamie snapped, embarrassed. "It's stupid. Forget it."

Lauren looked at him. "You mean so you can provide me with your incredible wealth of editing experience?"

"Yeah." Jamie nodded. "Something like that. It would be a great excuse to—uh—keep on seeing you."

"I see," Lauren replied, holding back, knowing that it was Dash she cared about. Jamie was her friend, but he'd never be more than that.

"But maybe we could keep seeing each other anyway," Jamie said cautiously, leaning forward, trying to catch her eye. "I mean, I've got to be honest with you, Lauren. I think I spent a lot of time on that story for you. Not for the magazine. Not for me. But for you."

Lauren looked up, biting back tears. What Jamie didn't realize was that she hadn't done the story for herself.

She'd written it for Dash.

Jamie was nervously thumbing the corner of her article, staring at the potted plant in the corner of the room.

"Look, Jamie."

"Why do I have the feeling you're not going to extend your internship?" Jamie said, one eyebrow raised.

"It's not that I haven't been tempted to get involved with you," Lauren began, staring at the minute stitches in the strap of her purse. "I like you a lot—"

"It probably hit you the night I steadied your bowling ball and called you honey," Jamie broke in.

Lauren didn't smile. "It's Dash. I need to find out where we're going."

"Ah, yes. Dash." Jamie sighed. "Your other editor."

"I wrote that story for him, Jamie. I still care about him a lot."

"Okay." Jamie nodded sadly.

Lauren looked over at his patient face. He'd been kind to her. He'd given her the biggest break of her career so far. "But if things don't work out," Lauren said gently, "you'll be the first person I'll call."

"Good," Jamie said with mock seriousness. He stood up and walked around his desk. Then he took her hand in his. "Look, about the byline. It's your story. I'm not going to share it with you."

"But your research . . ." Lauren started to protest.

Jamie shook his head slowly as he pulled her up with his hand. "I'll do a sidebar on the small-town gang stats. It'll work."

"Okay," Lauren barely whispered. Jamie's face was so near. There was so much energy and passion in it.

"Would you let me kiss you, Lauren?" Jamie whispered. "It looks like this is good-bye. And I . . ."

Without hesitating, Lauren lifted her lips and kissed him softly as his arms encircled her waist. It was a friendly kiss. A kiss between friends. A farewell.

"Good-bye, Jamie," Lauren said with a clutch in her throat. "I've enjoyed every moment I've spent with you. Including the last one."

Eighteen

KC headed quickly up the brick stairs to the Tri Beta house's shiny green front door Monday morning. Inside, the front entryway was covered with paint-spattered canvas, and two workmen on ladders were carefully steadying a massive chandelier back into place.

Clutching her briefcase, KC tiptoed down the hall to the kitchen, which was now repaired and painted. Fresh curtains fluttered around the windows, and an electrician had just finished reinstalling a light fixture over the Tri Beta's large meeting table.

"Must be nice to have everything back to

normal," the electrician said, cheerfully snapping his tool chest shut.

"Yes," KC lied politely.

"Nice evening." He tipped his hat and left.

"Yeah," KC murmured, dropping her briefcase down on the table with a thud. The kitchen looked like the same old kitchen. But so what? Everything else had completely changed.

KC heard a footstep at the door and looked up.

It was Courtney.

For a moment, Courtney just stood in the doorway, looking hurt and confused. Since Saturday's humiliating meeting, Courtney had all but disappeared. Now her face looked pale, and her jaw was locked into an expression of silent pain.

"Hi," KC said quietly.

Courtney gripped her notebooks closer to her chest. "Hello."

KC drew out a chair and sat down in it. "I came early, Courtney, because I needed to talk with you about something."

Courtney didn't move. Her eyes drifted wearily out the window. "What about? Money? The way I spent my time reading to a bunch of poor kids yesterday?"

"No, Courtney, I didn't come here to talk about the Tri Betas or complain about you."

"Good," Courtney came back quickly. She walked over to the table, sat down facing KC, and folded her slender hands in front of her. In the

"We both would," KC said sadly, "if she comes back."

Courtney sat up straight. "You know what we could do with the gazebo money, KC? We could put it into an emergency medical fund for Annie. Or maybe for any other girl who needs it."

KC nodded without saying anything.

"I know," Courtney went on, sobbing. "I know everyone thinks I've forgotten them. But I care too much about everything going on around me. And what I see isn't good. I see our girls burned out of their home by a vicious hate group. I see children who don't have enough to eat. People dying of a terrible disease. Don't you see? I can't just sit back anymore, KC. I can't ignore it."

Trembling and exhausted, KC stood up and walked around the table. Then she sat down next to Courtney and hugged her gently. "You're right not to ignore it."

"Maybe I've gone too far," Courtney said tearfully. "But I can't help it."

"We'll meet you halfway," KC said with conviction, realizing that she meant every word. "We've got our heads in the sand here, and you're going to help us pull out."

Courtney looked at her, hopeful.

"I'm sorry, Courtney," KC said, quietly bowing her head. "We had a disagreement, sure. But I never wanted it to get out of control like this. I never wanted to be pitted against you."

Courtney sniffed and looked up. "You're the best friend I have on this campus, Angeletti," she said. "You'd better not desert me now."

KC gave her a sad smile. "Just go easy on us, Courtney. You're the visionary. Okay? So just give the rest of us mortals a little time to catch up."

"Agreed," Courtney muttered, dropping her head down tiredly on KC's shoulder, just as a group of Tri Beta sisters arrived through the kitchen door. "Anything to pull this group back together. We need each other, KC. We need each other more than we're willing to admit. Maybe that's what Annie has shown us."

KC and Courtney huddled closer, quietly talking. Slowly, the rest of the Tri Betas began to file into the kitchen, and KC sensed the impact they were having on the other sisters.

It was clear the feud was over. And it was clear, from the looks of surprise and relief they were getting, that everyone else was as glad as they were.

Nineteen

KC lay alone on her narrow bed in Langston House, staring at the candle-light fluttering along the cracks of the empty ceiling.

She gazed at her bare walls and the calendar on her bulletin board. The room was still as sterile and empty as it had been the first day she moved in last fall. And now Annie's cot was gone.

Now Annie was gone.

KC sighed, stood up, and looked out over the dorm green. That morning, Annie had left in a taxi, taking with her a small mountain of off-beat belongings.

KC pressed her cheek against the glass, gazing at

a couple kissing under a tree near a campus pathway.

She bit the corner of her lip, looking away. Two days ago, she'd been like a house on fire, waiting for Cody, longing for Cody, planning for Cody. Today, everything was different.

Turning away, KC walked a few steps back and looked at her face in the mirror. Annie's news had shaken her badly. She'd spent most of the night crying into her pillow. But there was something else, too. KC suddenly wondered if her urgency about Cody had had a lot to with Annie.

Maybe she secretly longed for something Annie had. Adventure. Freedom. Passion. Maybe that was what she thought she'd find if she slept with Cody. But she couldn't really remember now. Because everything had changed.

Someone knocked on her door.

KC got up slowly and padded toward it. She knew it was Cody. After all, this was the day—the night—they'd sort of talked about. The night they would spend together for the first time.

"Hi," Cody said, handing her a single white tulip. His dark-brown hair was pulled back straight off his face, and his deep eyes seemed to be looking right into the middle of her heart.

"Thanks." KC took the flower, then turned away. Somehow, being with Cody right now was strange. "Where—where did you get this?" She stared at the flower, not knowing what to do with it.

"From the Peabody House garden," Cody said,

sitting down on her bed. He rolled up the sleeves of his denim shirt, then rested his elbows thoughtfully on his knees. "You look terrible."

"Thanks." KC walked numbly over to the window and pressed her nose to the pane. It was staying light late now, and the silky smell of the river cottonwoods was floating in on the evening air. "It smells good, doesn't it?" KC said quietly, sliding the window open farther. "I never noticed it before. Annie pointed it out to me. The smell of the cottonwoods."

"I hope she comes back," Cody said. "We need more people like her around."

"I guess she's home now."

Cody rolled onto his side on the bed. "Must be."

"I—I wonder how she told her parents," KC couldn't help thinking out loud. She dug her knuckles into her forehead. "From what Annie told me, they're really great people."

"Good. She'll need support and love." Cody patted the spot next to him on KC's bed. "Come here."

KC sat down obediently, then scooted back and drew her knees up to her chest. Slowly, she began picking at the tiny shreds along the tear in her blue jeans.

"Having a hard time?" Cody asked, stroking one of her bare feet.

"Yeah," KC whispered. "I want to cry all the time."

"Look," Cody began, "I know we sort of made a date. But a lot has happened. You may not feel the same way."

"I'm scared, Cody. I wanted to really connect with

you—to make love and sleep with you for the whole night and forget everything else. Just you and me."

"And now?" Cody asked gently, holding her back a little so that he could look into her eyes. KC sighed. He didn't look angry. He looked as if he understood before she even said it.

"And now . . ." KC took a deep breath. "And now I'm not sure what I was longing for. Maybe I was just looking for a safe place. Maybe I was just trying to put out the fire."

"I know."

"When I found out about Annie," KC said, trembling, "it made me realize that even that wasn't safe. I mean, people all over the world are dying every day because they had sex and they weren't careful." KC dropped her head down and sobbed. "Isn't there anything left that's sacred? That's safe? I don't know what I think anymore."

"KC, KC," Cody murmured in her ear, stroking her long hair and holding her tight. "It's okay. There's no pressure. Please. I care about you. I love you. There's no way we're going to do anything just because we said we were."

"Then—then it's okay?" KC looked up timidly. "I mean, you understand? I don't want to rush into this. I want to know what I'm doing."

Cody held her close. "I'll wait. I'll do anything. I don't want this to be an escape. I want it to be much more than that."

Here's a sneak preview of
Freshman Passion, *the twenty-seventh*
book in the compelling story of
FRESHMAN DORM.

"You know," Winnie confided, "there are times when I just feel a little over-whelmed about being pregnant. Or maybe I should be honest and say *a lot* over-whelmed. Sometimes, I feel so happy. But then I crash, and I feel so tired I can barely move."

Dr. Schroeder smiled. "It's very simple. When you're tired, you should sleep. But . . . Winnie, I sense that something else is bothering you."

Winnie swallowed and nodded. "It's my friends. I can't talk to them about all this stuff—which is just about all I think of these days. They just don't relate."

"Well, why should they?" Dr. Schroeder replied.

"Pregnancy feels very far away to them. It's not part of their world yet."

"I know, but sometimes I think the rest of the U of S students think pregnancy is some kind of fatal disease. I mean, even Josh gets flipped out by it sometimes."

"Hmm. Do you think your husband isn't supportive of you?"

Winnie thought hard, then shook her head. "I guess not. I mean, he certainly tries hard. But the whole thing doesn't seem completely real to him. These days he only gets excited about that dumb motorcycle of his."

"He owns a motorcycle?" Dr. Schroeder looked alarmed. "And do you ride with him?"

Winnie shifted in her seat. "I don't like to, but I do because we don't have a car. Oh, but we wear crash helmets," she added quickly.

Dr. Schroeder shook her head. "Helmet or no helmet, pregnancy and motorcycles do not mix. Aside from the danger of an accident, the strong vibrations from the motor can affect the fetus. You know, more fetuses are lost in the first trimester— the first three months of pregnancy—than all other times put together. You need to be good to your body—and to the little life growing inside you."

Winnie shifted again. "I've told Josh I'd like him to sell it. I really have. But he won't." She looked sadly into Dr. Schroeder's face. "I don't want to nag him too much. It's already starting to feel like we're some bored, middle-aged couple."

For weeks, Winnie had been trying not to admit it to herself, but now that she'd said the words out loud, she knew she'd never be able to ignore the problem again.

Dr. Schroeder got up, walked over to Winnie, and placed a sympathetic hand on her shoulder. "Let's make a deal. Promise me you won't go riding on any more motorcycles, and I'll do a simple test that I think might help Josh relate a little more to what's going on inside your body."

Winnie didn't have to think twice. "No problem. I promise."

She had to get Josh to dump his motorcycle—and pronto.